Crossing
THE RAINBOW BRIDGE

Your Pet: When It's Time to Let Go

ROBERT SCOTT

ISBN: 1456403222
ISBN-13: 9781456403225
LCCN: 2010917785

AUTHOR'S NOTE

Dogs ask for very little: a pat on the head, a kiss on the nose, a pat on the butt, a partner to romp and play fetch with, and a full belly at mealtime. There's little else a dog requires. A dog lives to please its master for the time God gives them to share their lives together. In many relationships with a dog (or other pet), however, there comes a time we must let go. Humans can be selfish. We think we are doing our best friend a favor by extending its life when there is no hope. Learn a lesson from your pet. Learn when it's time. Then "let go." I learned this in hindsight. When *is* it time to let go? Watch your pet ... listen to your pet. Your pet will tell you.

—Robert Scott

DEDICATION

This book is dedicated to Foxy Lady III and the two fox terriers who preceded her, Foxy Lady and Foxy Lady II; Heidi and Heidi II, two schnauzer friends; and Tammy, a mutt who provided me with twenty years of pure joy. They are the ladies of my life: so much love was given to them, yet oh so much more was returned.

ACKNOWLEDGEMENTS

My heartfelt thanks go to Frank Kale, my best friend over a lifetime, for his encouragement, urging me on to make this book a reality in the midst of a broken heart and to author Bobbi Erhart (*Paper or Plastic: Life in the Check-Out Lane*, PublishAmerica) for her support. Special thanks to the staff of the animal hospital, especially Kaitlin and Gretchen who labored with such fervor in an attempt to save Foxy Lady III and for the love they provided when it was finally time for me to let go.

TABLE OF CONTENTS

CHAPTER I

Closing Day

As they left the bank, the faces of the young couple radiated with both happiness and relief. They had just finished the process of closing on their first home in Venice, Florida. Almost everything was ready for their wedding, which was less than three weeks away. The planning had been flawless, but planning didn't guarantee that the event would be perfect.

Dodging traffic, they headed to Dan's car to go for a late celebratory lunch at a famous tourist trap overlooking the Gulf of Mexico. Cathy looked radiant in her casual attire. As Dan opened her door, they quickly kissed, got into the car, and drove off. It was a typical Southwest Florida day—not a cloud in the sky, temperature approaching ninety, and extremely humid. But much of the humidity would be lost at the beach with the never-ending Gulf breeze.

"I'm so happy," Cathy said, bubbling like a child, checking out a treasure of trick-or-treat goodies on Halloween night. "It's really happening! We're going to be married and in our own home!"

"Yep, it's happening," Dan replied, "And so is all the work involved with moving, and that means that

I'll need to install a doggie-door for Cosmo from the kitchen to the lanai. There will be a lot more work to be done on our 'American Dream.' There are always things that are overlooked in the excitement of looking at a home, but they're sure to pop up once we're in there. We're fortunate, you know. Not many couples in their early- to mid-twenties can say that they have their own home."

He'd said it … he brought up the dog. Cathy wasn't too thrilled about immediately inheriting a family, especially a canine member, on the most important day of her life. But, she admitted to herself, *Cosmo has been with Dan since his high school days back in the '50s, and Dan really did love that dog.* And, she reminded herself, *He is a sweet dog.*

"Danny, how many dogs have you had in your lifetime?" she asked.

"Only two," he replied. "I got my first dog when I was about six. I wanted a Saint Bernard but my folks nixed that idea and brought a mutt home instead … a small mutt at that. They must have realized that they'd do most of the poop-scooping, at least until I was properly trained for the task. Sadie died when I was about fourteen. She was only eight years old. I cried for weeks afterward. I couldn't even go to school for several days. I remember my mom saying, 'Honey, it will get easier. I promise. You'll see Sadie again when you meet in heaven.'

"Of course I never believed that. My mom was just being kind, trying to console me. I've always had this inner conflict regarding my own beliefs and those I was taught by the church. My own thoughts seem real to me while "doctrine" and "dogma" seem like fairy tales. I could never accept many of the church's teachings that my faith told me that I must believe in order to get to a heaven that I don't truly believe in. I only kept practicing my religion for my folks' sake. I guess I need proof. Faith alone doesn't do it for me. My folks would be crushed if I ever walked away from something they are so strongly rooted in. Anyway, I got Cosmo less than a year after Sadie's death. He was only eight weeks old when I got him."

"I'm so sorry. It must have been difficult for you as a teenager, losing your best friend," Cathy replied as they reached the beach, parked and headed for the outside dining area. Cathy's parents were already seated, awaiting the soon-to-be newlyweds.

Cathy glanced toward Dan thinking, *His jet-black hair is the blackest I've ever seen and his green eyes are simply piercing. He is a handsome man.*

✍

"Well, it's about time," said Anne, Cathy's mother. "We thought we misunderstood you, and we'd have to stay until dinnertime." Anne was a class act. She could have passed for an older Grace Kelly. Casually dressed in an off-the-shoulder midriff and skin-tight Capri pants, not a blonde hair out of place and model-perfect makeup, she was a complete contrast to Bill, the father of the bride. A head full of nearly pure white hair rested under his visor. That visor, along with a loud flowered Hawaiian shirt and Bermuda shorts, shouted to the world that he'd just finished eighteen holes at a nearby golf course.

Cathy kissed her parents on the cheek as she picked up a menu and began reading it. Dan excused himself to go to the men's room.

"Oh Mom, I'm so happy. I don't think I've ever been happier in my life! Just think! Soon I'll be an old married woman, just like you!"

"Bite your tongue, young lady," countered Anne. "And please dear, call me 'Anne,' especially in public!"

Dan rejoined them moments later, and they ordered their late lunch and continued discussing plans for the upcoming big day and their plans for life in general. It was a good day, a near-perfect day, and hopefully it would set the course for a lifetime.

After an extended lunch, Anne and Bill returned home to get ready for an engagement that evening.

Dan and Cathy continued to discuss their plans. When they left the restaurant they drove to their new home to make notes of things that would need to be attended to before the wedding day.

❧

After graduating from college, both Cathy and Dan landed jobs working for a local newspaper. Cathy worked in the Photon department while Dan worked in display advertising. The jobs didn't pay all that well considering their degrees, but jobs were not all that easy to come by, and working the same shift meant that they wouldn't need a second car … something they could ill afford with a mortgage to look forward to until 1994.

1994? It seemed a lifetime away … it was a lifetime away … thirty years away!

Thirty years away? Cathy thought. *It will be a good life!*

Dan dropped her off at her parents' home and after a lingering kiss, drove off to his parents' home to get Cosmo. Then they left for the new home where he and Cosmo would live and he'd begin repairing to ready the house for the big day. "It will be a good life," he said aloud, almost as if he had heard Cathy think those same words only moments before. Cosmo looked at Dan, head cocked to one side with a quizzical expression on his face, as dogs so often do.

They pulled into the shell driveway, got out of the car and entered the house. It had the look of a Key West-style home but it was a single story ranch. Although it was lovingly cared for, there were still things to be done that would personalize it to suit Cathy and Dan's tastes.

Dan chuckled to himself. Cosmo appeared to be in doggie heaven as he roamed from room to room in the little bungalow, exploring, sniffing for signs of invaders, inhaling its newness.

He spotted a gecko and took chase, but the little lizard had a mind of its own. It quickly disappeared into the fireplace in the living room. It was safe—for now.

"Careful sport," Dan admonished, "That gecko might have alligator friends, and you don't want to mess with those critters!"

Cosmo wagged his tail wildly as if he'd actually understood what Dan had said.

After the excitement of the chase passed, food was the most important thing on Cosmo's mind. Dan had forgotten to bring both food for himself and Cosmo's food and water dishes. They drove back to his mom and dad's, then back home. Dan was happy that they were still in Englewood, a mere ten-minute drive for him. They were about to move to St. Augustine, and that would have been an overnight trip. He smiled to himself as he considered the alternative trip. It had been a long day. It had been a good day.

CHAPTER 2

Tragedy Strikes

With the wedding day fast approaching, Dan spent most of his spare time working on the house: painting, trimming, maintaining the lawn, and more. Cathy joined him on weekends, directing the operations while hanging new curtains, washing the kitchen drawers and more "woman stuff." It was a fun time, but filled with hard work. Neither complained. The hard work would be well worth the effort.

Cosmo occupied much of his time trying to catch the elusive geckos that basked in the sunshine, in search of their next meal. He was not at all successful, yet he persisted in trying.

"It's starting to shape up," Dan said as he reviewed the new paint in the master bedroom. "It's starting to become 'our' home." Everything began to fall into place. They already had a phone installed, a new TV antenna adorned the fireplace chimney, and the utilities were transferred to Dan's name. "Only two more rooms after this," Dan said, turning a full circle and re-admiring the fresh, inviting look of the room.

Cathy nodded in agreement as she finished the remnants of a sandwich that she'd prepared for each of them along with other goodies placed into a picnic basket. "Umm hmm," she added, wiping her lip to remove a dab of mayonnaise.

"Good sandwich, delicious," Dan said, finishing his. "I can't wait for you to cook our first meal in our first home."

"And what would that first home-cooked meal be?" Cathy asked. "Fried chicken, lasagna, spaghetti, beans and dogs?" She chuckled as she contemplated her cooking skills. Anne really wasn't the domestic type. Cathy learned most of her culinary skills from Bill. He could make an ordinary hamburger as inviting as a steak: a true master.

"I dunno," Dan replied. "We'll have to come up with something special for you to work on. You don't mind cooking, do you?"

"'Course not. Not for you, Danny," she said as she kissed his paint-spattered forehead and brushed a few errant hairs back where they belonged.

They rolled up the soiled mats that covered the floor in the bedroom and took them into the bathroom, spreading them out on the floor and over the sink, tub, and commode in preparation for starting the job the next day.

"I wish there were a second bathroom in this house," Cathy said. "It would be a big help when we have a family. But, I guess we can't expect to have everything the first time around, can we?"

"True," added Dan, "but down the road we can always build out from the master bedroom to add another one. There certainly is enough of a backyard, and that one can be all ours, no sharing, and that can happen in time. Right now that would be a bit too much to try and tackle. We'll need to hire a professional to do a job like that, and I'm sure that they don't come cheap!"

Cathy nodded in agreement as she mentally pictured the job already finished, complete with a stained-glass window that would become the highlight of the new bathroom.

"In time," she sighed, "in time."

�֍

The sun was setting. It was time to call it a day. Picnic basket in hand, Dan held the front door open for Cathy as he prepared to take her back to her parents' home. Cosmo brushed by her, loping toward the car in the driveway. He spotted a gecko and, as he always did, once again took chase, running toward the street.

Dan and Cathy reacted in horror as they heard the blaring of a horn followed by the sickening screeching of brakes and a muffled thump. It was Cosmo. He had been struck by an oncoming car in his quest to corral the gecko.

He lay in the street as the driver of the car got out and ran to him.

"Oh my God! Cosmo!" Dan screamed, dropping the picnic basket and running to the street. Cathy was right behind him.

"I am so sorry," the driver of the car said. "Your dog came out of nowhere. I tried to stop but it ran too fast. I am so sorry. I'm so sorry!"

"Quick," Dan shouted to Cathy. "Go look up the address and number of the nearest veterinarian. Go! Go! Go!" Dan knelt beside his canine friend, gently patting Cosmo, trying to comfort him. The dog was clearly in distress as a pool of blood formed under him.

The driver of the car continued to apologize but Dan paid no attention as he continued to comfort his friend.

Inside, a frantic Cathy flipped the phone book open to the Vs. She dialed the number of a veterinarian whose office was located less than two miles away. There was no answer. It was nearly 8:00 p.m., and a weekend. The office was closed.

"Damn! Damn!" she shouted in frustration at nobody in particular. Her fingers clumsily dialed the number of the police department. After what seemed like hours, a voice answered the phone.

"My dog was hit by a car," she screamed into the phone. "And the veterinarian's office is closed! Please, please, can you help?"

The officer gave her the name of an emergency clinic that catered to animals during "off hours." It was open from 5:30 p.m. until 8:00 p.m. weekdays and around the clock on weekends. It was less than a mile away. With shaking fingers she jotted down the address.

Cathy hung up without a word and ran back outside.

"There's an emergency clinic not far from here," she told Dan. "Get Cosmo in the car. I'll drive."

As she ran to the driver's side, the nameless man who had hit Cosmo handed her a piece of paper. "My name, address and phone number," he apologetically mumbled. "If there's anything that I can do …"

Cathy offered a quick "Thanks" as she hopped into the car and sped off in the direction of the clinic.

"Oh my God, oh God, oh God," Dan said, tears now streaming down his cheeks. "Oh, Cosmo!"

Driving as carefully as possible, Cathy was aware that she had exceeded the speed limit several times as they drove to the clinic. *Oh dear God, I hope we get there in time*, she thought to herself. Tears welled in her eyes as she realized how much Dan was hurting and how seriously Cosmo appeared to be injured. *This can't be happening!*

They reached the veterinarian's. As Cathy held the door open, Dan rushed past her with Cosmo in his arms. Blood was caked on Dan's paint-spattered T-shirt and shorts and was now running down his legs.

☙❧

"How can I help you?" asked the receptionist, not looking up. "Oh my … oh!" she said as she glanced upward. "Please, follow me!"

She led the couple into an examination room and laid a crisp paper sheet atop the exam table. "Put the poor dear down here," she said. "The doctor will be with you in a moment!"

"I'm Cathy," Cathy volunteered. "This is my fiancé, Dan Cooper, and our dog, Cosmo."

Dan gently placed Cosmo on the table, tears now flowing freely. "Oh Cosmo! Oh dear God, help us!" Dan found himself pleading to a God whose existence he had issues in believing.

Cathy stood beside him, shaking; wishing that she was capable of providing the comfort Dan was seeking, sobbing in an eerie unison with him, both imploring God for mercy.

The vet entered the room and began a preliminary exam, first applying his stethoscope to Cosmo's heart, then a various points on the chest.

"We'll need to take some X-rays," the doctor said with a troubled expression on his face. "The heart appears strong, but there could be internal injuries."

"Whatever," Dan said, "Do whatever needs to be done. Please ... oh please!"

An aide appeared and shifted Cosmo's limp body onto another table and wheeled it into another room.

"It will be a few minutes," said the vet. "You can stay in here, or if you prefer, in the reception room."

"We'll stay here," Cathy replied for both. "Thank you."

They both watched the second hand of the large clock on the wall. Tick, tock, tick, tock. It was an eternity. Less than five minutes had passed since Cosmo had been taken for the X-rays, but it seemed like hours had already gone by.

"Oh Cath," sobbed Dan, "it doesn't look good, does it?"

Cathy hesitated to respond, wishing this would all turn out to be a bad dream from which she'd awaken—from which Dan would awaken. She didn't want to say anything that might dash Dan's hopes. Inwardly she admitted to herself that it did not look good at all.

Instead of answering, Cathy gently brushed back Dan's hair and massaged his temples. Dan placed his hands over hers and gently intertwined his bloodied fingers with hers. Dan had not taken the time to wash his hands. He was too preoccupied with Cosmo's welfare.

As Cathy reached into her purse for a handkerchief, she found the scrap of paper that held the name, address, and phone number of the stranger who had hit Cosmo.

She tossed it into a wastebasket in the corner of the room while thinking, *It's really nobody's fault. It's something that happened. It was meant to be. What good would be accomplished by involving another person? More hurt, that's all!*

Tick, tock, tick tock: The clock on the wall continued its monotonous drone. Seven minutes had passed. Or had it been seven hours?

Night fell. Other than Cathy and Dan, along with the clinic's staff, there wasn't another soul in the building. *Thank heaven for that*, Cathy thought. *It would be difficult to have to see another animal in pain.* She grasped Dan's hands so tightly that she could see them turning white. She released the pressure and instead stroked his hands. His sobbing had subsided. He was silently crying as if he were resigning himself to the fact that he was losing Cosmo forever.

They both looked up abruptly at the sound of a "woof" from behind the closed door. It wasn't Cosmo. It was another patient that had awakened and was searching for something unseen, unknown, or perhaps it was a reaction to a doggie dream.

At last the door opened and the vet walked in, closely followed by the aide.

"It doesn't look good, Mr. Cooper," said the vet as he placed a series of X-rays onto a lighted panel for review. "There are numerous internal injuries, and as good as Cosmo's heart appears to be, I don't think that he'd survive multiple surgeries. He's simply lost too much blood."

Tears continued to flow from both Dan and Cathy's eyes as they realized the severity of the injuries.

"Can't anything be done?" Dan asked. "Can anything at all be done?"

"I'm so sorry, Mr. Cooper. He's beyond help."

"May we please see him again?" Dan asked

"Of course Mr. Cooper. Please follow me."

As they entered the room where Cosmo was X-rayed, the dog slowly lifted his head a mere fraction of an inch and briefly glanced in their direction. Then, just as quickly, his head dropped, eyes remaining open. Cosmo was gone.

The vet applied the stethoscope to his chest and probed for a heartbeat for a few seconds before saying, "I'm so sorry, Mr. Cooper."

"No! Damn it, no! He can't be gone—not like this. He should have lived for years longer." Dan's grief was uncontrollable. Tears began again as he held the dog in a tight, yet gentle grip. Cathy, across the table from him was sobbing.

"Would you like to stay with him for a while?" asked the vet. "Gretchen," he said to the aide, "Would you please bring Mr. Cooper and his fiancée some coffee?"

"Of course," the aide replied, quietly exiting the room.

"Thank you," Dan replied to the vet. "Yes, we would like to be with him for a while."

Dan patted Cosmo's head as he continued to sob. "This never should have happened. It was my fault! I should have been more careful. I know how he was with geckos. He loved to chase them. Oh Cathy, Cosmo is gone because of me!"

"Danny, I am so sorry, honey. All things happen for a reason. We don't know what the reason is, but apparently this was meant to be. Nothing that you or I did caused this. It was a freak accident. We did everything that we could, and we were not successful. But honestly, we can't blame ourselves. Cosmo was meant to live until today and no amount of rationalizing or pleading or bargaining with God can change that. Trust that I am hurting as much as you are." Again she brushed his hair back to where it belonged and gently kissed the top of his head. Cathy shared the fierce pain of loss, yet she attempted to provide the strength that Dan needed and she was determined not to fail him.

"I know, Cath. I know that in my mind, but it's my heart that is broken." The tears continued to flow.

Less than a half-hour later they were headed back to the house. The vet's staff had transferred Cosmo's body into a corrugated cardboard box. They would bury him at home, in the backyard, that night; the only light to dig his grave would be the brilliant light of a June moon that seemed all that much brighter in Florida. It would turn out to be a long, long day: a day that started so carefree yet ended with an inconsolable sadness. Cosmo was gone forever. Like Sadie before him, however, he would never be forgotten. Unlike with Sadie, Dan would have a bride to mourn with him. A person should never have to mourn alone. The death of a dog, a friend, should be mourned just as well as a human.

As Dan began to dig the grave, Cathy gathered Cosmo's toys, leash, collar, and tags and lovingly placed them around the beautiful bundle of fur. She then took the dog's favorite blanket and gently covered him and tucked it in as if to prepare a child for a good night's sleep.

Dan replaced the lid atop the corrugated box and together they lowered it gently into the freshly dug grave.

"Wait!" said Cathy, as she ran to the front of the house. She returned in a few minutes with a bouquet of fresh flowers picked from a small bed at the front porch and placed them on top of the box.

"Goodbye Cosmo," Cathy offered. "Until we meet again in heaven."

"I truly wish that I had the faith that you have in believing that," added Dan. "Goodbye my dear and faithful friend. You will be sorely missed."

Dan filled the grave. It was over.

Cathy decided that she would stay at the house that night. It had been a long, long day. A beautiful day that suddenly turned horribly tragic.

The next morning, as she glanced out the kitchen window she noticed something on top of the grave. As she walked out the back door and approached it she read the small engraved wooden plaque:

Cosmo
Loving Friend and Companion
1955–1964

"I worked on it while you were sleeping," a red-eyed Dan confessed as he walked to stand behind Cathy, hands on her shoulders. "It's crude, carved with my old Boy Scout knife, but it will serve its purpose. A friend as faithful as Cosmo should not have to spend eternity in an unmarked grave."

Cathy nodded in silent, loving agreement. Inside, her heart was heavy however she continued to be the rock that Dan needed. She forced herself to hold back the tears that began to sting her eyes.

A few days later, Dan found a blank envelope behind the flag on the mailbox. Opening it, he read:

"I'm the man who hit your dog. I didn't want you to think that it meant nothing to me. I called the vet's office to ask about the dog's condition and they told me that your dog did not survive. I am so sorry. Please let me know if there's anything that I can do for you." The man's name and phone number appeared, hastily scrawled, yet readable.

Dan read it a second time as he thought, *People are basically good.*

CHAPTER 3

The Wedding Day

Dan's parents arrived from their new home in St. Augustine a few days before the wedding. It turned out to be a whirlwind week of activities.

Millie Cooper was Bert's second wife. Dan's mother, Pam, died of leukemia when Dan was only four years old. Bert and Millie married three years later. But to anyone who saw them together, it was evident that Millie loved Dan as much as any natural mother could love her own. Bert and Millie didn't have any children together.

Bill, wearing his trademark loud floral Hawaiian shirt, Bermuda shorts, and ever-present visor, got fitted for a tuxedo at the rental store, and Anne, determined to outshine every woman at the church, shopped Sarasota and Venice until she found the dress that would make everyone stand up and take notice. And, that they did!

As guests filed into the church, Dan, stood secluded with his groomsmen in the sacristy, fidgeted with his tie, then with the peach colored rose in his lapel while wringing his hands together. As always, he felt uncomfortable being in a church but he did his best to ignore his discomfort.

"You're sure that you have the ring?" he asked his best man.

"Relax, Dan," his best friend from college replied. "It's right here—uh oh! Where is it? Omigosh! I lost the ring!" Before Dan had a chance to get upset, he added, "Just kidding pal! Here it is," as he held up the symbol of infinity that would soon bind Dan and Cathy for life.

"Great, thanks man," said Dan as he feigned wiping a brow full of sweat with the palm of his hand. The wedding had to be perfect. Of course it wouldn't make the press like the wedding of Grace Kelly and Prince Rainier had only eight years earlier, but this was their day. It belonged to Cathy and Dan. It had to be perfect.

Dan glanced out of the sacristy. He could only see the first few rows, but he beamed when he saw his parents and Cathy's mom across the aisle. Dressed to the nines, they looked so proud and so happy.

And he was proud of them—all of them. He was thrilled that even though his own mother couldn't be with them, Millie, whom he loved dearly, made a perfect stand-in for her. His dad was a hard-working laborer, yet looking every bit the successful businessman in his tux. It made a great picture. He hoped that the photographer got some pictures of them sitting there. He'd want them for his kids; for his grandkids.

It was time. The priest ushered the men out of the sacristy to take their places at the altar. Then he joined them.

The soft strains of the organ signaled the bride's entrance. With an arm entwined in her dad's, Cathy began her walk with Bill down the aisle, led by a diminutive flower girl who concentrated on tossing peach-colored rose petals one by one onto the carpet from a basket that was filled to the brim.

"Dad," Cathy whispered as they walked down the aisle, "You do look handsome in your tux. I was fully convinced that you might show up wearing a Hawaiian shirt, Bermuda shorts, and your visor. That's the dad I know and love so much, but I love your formal look."

Bill simply smiled as he patted her arm.

A bit concerned that she might run out of petals before reaching the altar, the flower girl seemed to hoard them until someone, perhaps her own mother, whispered something to her as she passed by. She then began tossing them out freely by the handful. It was a precious thing to see—an innocent child leading the way toward the start of a new life for the happy couple.

Dan fairly beamed as Cathy seemed to fairly float down the aisle. He was so in love with her. He promised himself that he would never do anything to knowingly hurt her. She was his reason for living.

"Who gives this woman …?" asked the priest, as he had done hundreds of times over the course of his priesthood.

"I do," a glowing Bill said as her placed Cathy's hand in Dan's. He kissed Cathy on the cheek. As he began to turn away, a single tear formed on Bill's cheek. He'd leave it there. It was a tear of joy; a good tear. It belonged. As Bill took his seat, Dan saw a series of flashbulbs pop. He was immensely pleased. The photographer was on the ball!

The small reception was flawless. After numerous toasts to the bride and groom, Millie stood before a podium and said, "One final toast, please. Hush everyone."

Dan fidgeted as he hoped that she hadn't had too much to drink. Only one champagne could set her off—nothing nasty or mean, but after a few drinks she would talk forever. She had little tolerance for alcohol, but she loved Bert too much to risk abusing it and embarrassing him.

"To Dan's mother, Pam, who could not be here with us today. She had a previous engagement in heaven, but rest assured that she's watching from afar," she said as she raised the remains of the glass of club soda, the only thing that she'd had to drink. "To Pam!"

"To Pam!" the small crowd echoed as in one voice.

Dan smiled broadly and said, "Thanks, Mom!" then he kissed her on the cheek. The moment was somber and glorious at the same time.

Cathy then rose and said, "And one more. Here's a toast to a dear friend Cosmo, who would also have loved to share this day. He also had a prior engagement—in doggie heaven."

Dan knew in that instant that there was no mistake. He'd chosen the right person to be his wife. His Cathy, his wife, his love and his life. They'd be together forever!

❦

The happy couple had decided when they bought their home that there would not be a honeymoon. They would use those monies for advance payments on their mortgage, repairs and alterations to the house, and other essentials. That, they felt, was thinking ahead. Their plan was to save for a not-to-be forgotten honeymoon in Europe for their twenty-fifth anniversary—Paris, London, Rome, maybe even more. They had twenty-five years to plan for it.

And so, their life together began in a small Key West-style home in Venice. It was only twenty-four years and 364 days (or so, allowing for leap years) from their twenty-fifth anniversary. A lot could happen in twenty-four years and 364 days (or so, allowing for leap years), and a lot would happen.

CHAPTER 4

"I'm Pregnant!"

"Are you okay, hon?" a concerned Dan said to Cathy as he dressed for work. She'd been in the bathroom vomiting for what seemed like hours.

"I'm fine," she replied, emerging from the bathroom, "but I don't know if you will be."

"Whatcha mean, Cath?"

"Danny, I think I might be pregnant. I've been feeling sick for the past few days, mostly first thing in the morning. I made an appointment with the doctor. I won't be going in to work today. I didn't say anything before because I didn't want to worry you."

"Worry me? Cath, that's great news! If it's true, I'm thrilled! Want me to go to the doctor with you?"

"No, that's fine. If I am pregnant, you'll need to be the breadwinner in this household until I can return to work."

Dan reopened the bathroom door, and as the light from the stained-glass window beamed on her face, Cathy looked like an angel, standing there, stroking an imaginary oversized tummy.

"I might become a mommy! I really might!" she said.

"And I might be a daddy," Dan said excitedly, placing his hand on her perfectly flat tummy in order to feel the baby kicking.

"You'd better get moving along, Daddy. We'll need that money for diapers, formula, and a million other things that go along with having a baby … and … have you even considered turning the second bedroom into a nursery?" It was obvious that both of them were extremely happy. She said, "I'll call you at work as soon as I get back from the doctor, Daddy. I promise! Now get moving and while I think of it, if I am pregnant, you might want to formulate the words that you want to use to ask Hoskins for a raise! Tell him that raising a child is a bit different than raising a potted plant!"

CHAPTER 5

A Family of Three

William Bertram Cooper entered the world in February, 1967. His parents agreed that "Junior" simply would not work. He was named in honor of his maternal grandfather. He was an average-sized newborn with a shock of hair that rivaled his dad's. And he was no sissy. It took three slaps on the butt to get him to cry.

"I'm so proud of you, Cath. You were a real trooper at the hospital," Dan said as he admiringly watched Cathy nurse their son in the newly renovated second bedroom of their Key West-style home. He was with Cathy as she gave birth, and he envied her fortitude and strength when he felt like he was going to pass out from the ordeal.

"I'm proud of you too, hon, for making this nursery a room that any little boy would envy. It's simply perfect. The boating/fishing motif is the ideal touch," she replied.

The moment of reverie was briefly interrupted as a four-month-old Billy burped, then spit out the last few ounces of his dinner. They laughed aloud as he produced a burp that a Japanese sumo wrestler at a state dinner might consider worthy of a bow at the waist.

"He's his father's son," Cathy said proudly. Right down to the last burp!

Dan smiled broadly as he took Billy from her arms and washed his smiling, gurgling mouth and the last remnants from his chin.

"He's our son," Dan countered. "Our perfectly beautiful son, who just happens to take after his dad. Sorry, but I see it more each day."

"Not to worry," Cathy replied. "Our daughter will take after me."

"You're not," Dan replied. "So soon?"

"No, relax hon. I was only kidding with you. But you never know when that could happen."

However, Billy would be the only child for the couple.

CHAPTER 6

"I Want a Puppy"

It was bound to happen. It's a part of being human. All little boys want a dog, and Billy was a perfectly normal kid. Shortly before his sixth birthday, Billy asked Dan and Cathy if he could have a dog. He wanted a wire-haired fox terrier "just like the one I saw on TV." He wanted a female. He even had her name picked out: Foxy Lady. He had it all worked out. He was a smart kid. After all, he was the product of Cathy and Dan.

"Please," he begged. "Everyone should have a dog. Dad, didn't you have dogs when you were a kid?"

How could so heartwarming a plea be dismissed? Of course, Dan and Cathy agreed after providing Billy with a crash course centering on the responsibilities and care involved in having a puppy.

"Fox terriers are really hard to come by here in Florida," Dan explained. "We'll have to advertise for one. And Billy, you never know what their background might be. They might come from a puppy mill. That's a place where dogs are used for breeding, many times over their lifetime. They could inherit traits that could jeopardize them later in life. Are you sure that you want to do this? You must always be prepared for the sudden loss of a dog. That's a very unpleasant circumstance. It's terribly painful. I've been through it twice, and it never gets easier."

He went on to say, "Purebred animals like fox terriers, German Shepherds, and more can often be subject to illnesses that are specific to their breed. You might want to reconsider and get a 'mutt.' They generally don't suffer from specific diseases, and often in the long run, they live longer than purebreds."

"Nope! I want a fox terrier just like the one I saw on TV," the adamant child replied.

"You're sure that you are prepared to accept the bad times with the good?"

"Yes! Yes, I can do it! I can take care of a pup. She'll be my best friend forever," the boy answered.

And so it was, several weeks later in 1973, that a young "Foxy Lady Cooper" joined the Cooper family.

She was an adorable bundle of fur, an extremely active puppy, mostly white with a brown saddle spanning her back, matched by brown ears and a splotch of brown at the tip of her short cropped tail. She and Billy bonded instantly, as she did with Dan and Cathy. It had become one small happy family.

◦✺◦

Several weeks later, Billy joined Dan as he delivered Lady to the vet's office for the last of her "puppy" shots and, while there, made arrangements for Lady to be spayed when the time came. Since he had no intention of breeding her, Dan wanted to be certain that she couldn't fall victim to a stray marauding dog "having its way" with her. The visits would help Billy understand the many responsibilities of dog ownership.

❧

"It's good to see you again, Mr. Cooper," Gretchen, one of the vet's aides said, "under happier circumstances." She made an appointment for the date Lady would be spayed.

"Thanks, Gretchen," he said, surprised that she remembered him after all the years that had passed. "Yes, it's far more pleasant today," he said, accepting the appointment card.

Billy took his responsibilities very seriously indeed, and after only a few minor lapses, fully accepted his duties without the need to be reminded. He and Lady played together every chance they could, and she slept curled up in a doggie bed at the foot of his bed. That didn't last long, however.

One night when Billy was having a bad dream, an inquisitive Lady hopped up on his bed and began licking his face, waking the boy. After a few moments of play, she pawed and scratched around the covers for what seemed an eternity to create a comfy spot next to Billy, finally settling in a "spoon" position at his waist. She claimed the space. It was a position that she would assume each night at bedtime from that point on.

CHAPTER 7

School Begins

"Billy, it's time to stop playing with Lady and come in and finish your breakfast. The school bus will be here soon," Cathy reminded her son through the kitchen window. "You don't want to be late for your first day of school, do you?"

"Awww, Mom, already?" the boy asked. "What will Lady do all day while I'm at school?"

"Believe me, honey, she'll survive. She'll have some time to do nothing but nap and get rested up for when you return home. Dogs don't know what time means, and she'll be fine. You'll see!"

Lady led the way, passing through the doggie door as they entered the kitchen, stopping at her water dish for a few laps. Billy patted her on her head, then her butt as he kissed her cold damp nose goodbye.

"See ya later, Lady! Be a good girl and listen to Mom, ya hear?"

❧

A solitary dad stood on the corner with his daughter. The remainder of the small group consisted of mothers seeing their children off for their first day of school. It was a sweltering August morning. Cathy joined the group waiting for the school bus to arrive, admiring Billy who was sporting a light blue shirt, darker blue shorts, white socks, and deep blue sneakers. He certainly was his father's son. She could picture Dan and Millie standing on a similar street corner many years ago as he prepared for his first day of school.

She smiled a warm greeting toward the other parents. The bus had arrived and the children were boarding the bus, each child looking for the perfect seat that would be theirs for the remainder of the school year. It was a bittersweet morning. She spotted Billy as he claimed the last seat on the bus, kneeling on the seat and waving a goodbye to Lady and Mom as the bus rode off.

⚜

Cathy, along with a leashed Lady, stood waiting for the school bus that afternoon, along with the small group of mothers. Apparently the solitary dad from that morning worked an afternoon shift. An unrecognized woman had joined the group.

When the bus stopped, Cathy was able to determine that the "new" woman was the child's mother when the little girl hopped off the last step of the bus and ran to her mother, hugging her while exclaiming, "Mommy! I really liked school!"

Billy was the last of the children to exit the bus.

"Lady! I missed you, girl," he said excitedly, patting her on the head and eagerly accepting the barrage of kisses on his nose, cheeks, and forehead.

Cathy realized that she'd have to resign herself to becoming the "second fiddle" in his life, although he did volunteer the obligatory hug and kiss for Mom. Kids at that age aren't embarrassed to give Mom a hug and kiss.

Being embarrassed by a parental kiss in front of his peers is a learned action that Billy, too, will learn all too soon, Cathy thought and quickly dismissed it as a self-serving thought, not worthy of dwelling on.

Still on leash, Lady led the way back home, a short distance away, looking back every so often as if to be sure that Billy didn't disappear again.

After a few cookies and a glass of milk, Billy took Lady outside to play. Carefully guiding her still on the leash, he went to the front of the house.

Moments later, as Cathy glanced out the kitchen window, she could see Billy laying a small bunch of fresh flowers on Cosmo's grave. *How like his father,* she thought, *kind and considerate in every way.* She would have to remember to tell Dan of the sweet, heartwarming gesture when he returned from work.

CHAPTER 8

A Doggie Birthday

Life had changed dramatically in the year preceding Lady's eighth birthday. Dan's parents had both died months apart. His dad, Bert, who had just turned sixty-one, died of a massive heart attack in 1977. His stepmother, Millie, died less than a year later at age fifty-nine. Some thought that she'd died of a broken heart mourning the death of her husband. She'd lost all interest in life after Bert's death. Dan was able to cope and get on with his life by immersing himself in his work but their deaths affected Cathy to a greater degree. She was extremely fond of her in-laws and their passing reminded her of her own mortality. She often found herself wondering what would happen to Billy and Dan if she were to die unexpectedly, and although she tried to dismiss such thoughts, they continued to haunt her. She never shared those thoughts with Dan.

Dan was promoted in his job in 1979, and the couple sold their home and moved to a larger home in the same city. Billy was thrilled because the new home had a heated swimming pool that he and Lady enjoyed nearly all year, and Billy became quite the swimmer and diver.

Cathy discovered more of the depths of Billy's caring while unpacking in their new home as she opened a box and unwrapped a carefully packaged, faded, weather-beaten, yet readable plaque that had adorned Cosmo's gravesite. Billy had included a note, carefully taped to the back: "I figured that you'd want to take this reminder of Cosmo to the new house rather than have the new owners toss it in the trash," It read.

She felt a wave of pure love as she realized how much a "man" her son was becoming. She carefully rewrapped it, making a mental note to tell Dan. How proud he'd be of Billy.

Cathy was sad to leave their first home, but she was thrilled with the new modern kitchen, huge great room with fireplace, four bedrooms and 2.5 baths in their new home, along with something Dan had always wanted: a two-car attached garage and a storage shed for his tools, lawnmower and more. For Billy was the swimming pool that he and Lady so enjoyed.

For the most part, life had been good to them. Cathy left her job to become a full-time wife and mother. Both agreed it was a wise choice to call an end to her career, and she was happier than ever in her new role. Dan was even able to fit a second car into the budget so that Cathy didn't need to drive him to work in order to have the luxury of the use of an automobile. It was a used car, a sporty looking 1979 Chevrolet Camaro. It suited the thirty-seven-year-old Cathy well.

Billy constantly reminded her, "One day this car will be mine," wishing that "one day" would come soon and that Dan would buy Cathy a new car. He'd clearly be the envy of his classmates driving to school in those wheels! He still had several years to wait until he could get a driver's license.

Now in junior high, Billy was a valued member of his school's swim team. Lady was about to turn eight, according to the certification from the breeder and the American Kennel Club, and the family planned a small celebration in her honor.

Yes, all-in-all, life had moved along in a somewhat normal course for the Coopers, when considering that death is a part of life; however thoughts of an early death continued to plague Cathy.

❧

"Billy, get yourself together. Grandpa and Grandmom will be here soon," Cathy shouted from the kitchen. Her voice trailed through the huge great room and out onto the lanai right into the pool where Billy and Lady were enjoying a midsummer game of "catch the ball" under the hot Venice sun.

Billy had really sprung up in the past year, going from a lanky thirteen-year-old to a fit and trim four-teen-year-old, complete with a youthful, muscular swimmer's body. He went on his first date shortly after his last birthday. According to him, it was a "disaster." He proclaimed that he hated all girls and would forever … except for Lady. His date was the daughter of a prominent businessman and, truth be told, a spoiled little brat whose greatest pleasure was to put everyone down. There was a lesson somewhere there, begging to be learned. Hopefully it would be learned sooner than later. He hadn't dated since that night, preferring instead, to spend his time with Lady, in the pool doing laps and perfecting his dives.

"Okay, Mom! I'm on my way," he replied as he and Lady exited the pool. He quickly towel-dried her and both went to his bedroom through the slider on his side of the house where he showered and changed in preparation for his grandparents' arrival.

"That was fun, wasn't it girl?" he said to Lady. She, in turn, cocked her head to one side (as dogs do) as if to interpret what he'd just said. It didn't matter what he said, that he'd said it pleased her.

Emerging from his bedroom he padded barefoot into the kitchen where Cathy busied herself in putting the finishing touches on the menu.

❧

The eight-chime doorbell rang, and Billy went to answer the door with Lady trailing closely behind. "Grandpa, Grandmom," he said as he opened the door to let them in. Giving each a hug and kiss, he said, "It's great to see you! You both look wonderful! How was the drive?"

"Young man," Anne replied, "if anyone looks wonderful, you do! What have you done with yourself? The drive was fine. Uneventful and not too much traffic: That's something that I simply cannot cope with—traffic. People on the road nowadays are so inconsiderate

"Been keeping busy in the pool," he replied. "Lady, too. Doesn't she look great?" Lady's fur looked like mouton after it dried following the session in the pool, curly and tight, since Billy had failed to brush her before she dried.

"She's lovely," replied Anne, as Bill nodded in agreement. Lady seemed to sense the admiration as she bestowed a generous, sloppy kiss on both Anne and Bill's outstretched hands.

"You're turning into a fine young man, Billy," Bill said as they followed him into the kitchen.

"Mom, Dad," Cathy said as she welcomed both with a hug and kiss. "It's so good to see you. It's simply been too long."

Bill stretched out on a chaise enjoying a beer while Billy and Lady busied themselves on the lanai playing "catch." Cathy set the dining room table. Her mom followed dutifully behind, fixing the nonexistent errant folds of the napkins and making certain the silverware was "just so."

"Mom, President Reagan and Nancy aren't joining us for dinner tonight; they send their regrets. It's just going to be the five … uh, six of us, including Lady. No need for perfection," Cathy chuckled.

"Dear, when will you learn to call me 'Anne'?" she replied, laughingly. "I *am* 67 now, and if you continue to call me 'Mom' people will get the idea that I'm getting old."

"Mom, you'll always be younger than springtime … at least to me," Cathy replied, "and besides I'm proud that you're my mother, and there is not a soul here that cares how old you are, is there?"

"You're right dear … you usually are," Anne said.

Splash! The sound echoed throughout the house as Anne and Cathy looked toward the lanai. Lady had misjudged and while chasing the "catch" ball, she slipped into the pool.

Doggie-paddling toward the steps at the edge of the pool, Lady appeared to be smiling and saying, "I did that on purpose." Billy reached for a beach towel to dry her as she stepped onto the lanai from the top step.

She escaped the towel, instead shaking herself of the excess water, perfectly in line with Bill. As she shook her body, Bill said, "Awww, Lady! You just had to do that, didn't you?" He grinned at his grandson, adding, "That's some pooch you have there, son!"

Both chuckled, watching the dog attempt to shake herself dry. It was a good day.

"Happy birthday to you … happy birthday to you … happy birthday, dear Lady, happy birthday to you."

The chorus of five finished the musical interlude as a confused Lady cocked her head (as dogs so often do) in an attempt to understand what that was all about. Whatever it was, she enjoyed it.

The family headed to the dining room to enjoy their dinner, as Lady meandered into her "eating place" in the kitchen.

Her birthday meal, a combination of rice, hamburger, green beans, and carrots, with a dollop of cottage cheese mixed in, was too much for her to comprehend. She dug in furiously, finishing the feast before her family had completed their salads. It was an unexpected treat, and her doggie bowl was licked clean.

Birthday or not, Lady found life to be good.

There was no birthday cake that Lady would share. The family had a cake with chocolate icing. However, there was a special "doggie" ice cream served to the canines at the party. Well, one canine.

It was a good party. If turning eight meant a celebration like today's, turning nine would have to be even more special.

Unfortunately, turning nine was not in the cards for Foxy Lady.

CHAPTER 9

The News Is Not Good

The day after Lady's eighth birthday party was not a happy day. Lady didn't touch a bite of her breakfast, and she refused to join Billy in the pool at "catch" time. She simply was not herself, walking slowly and deliberately to get from here to there.

She dutifully did her "jobs," but there was something strange in her demeanor; a something that could not be pinpointed. Yet, it didn't appear that there was cause for concern.

"I'm sure that she'll be fine," Dan said. "The celebration might have been too much for her. You didn't give her any cake, did you Billy?"

"No," Billy replied. "I know that chocolate isn't good for dogs, and the icing was chocolate. The only thing that I gave her in addition to her dinner was that cup of puppy ice cream. And she ate all of that."

"Well," Dan said, "If she doesn't seem better, or if she doesn't eat her lunch, I'll make an appointment at the vet. Something is wrong with her."

Cathy, Dan, and Billy watched her carefully for the remainder of the weekend.

Monday came, and nothing had changed. Lady still hadn't eaten a full meal. She'd merely picked. She was drinking what appeared to be excessive amounts of water.

"I'll call the vet after you leave for school," Cathy said to Billy as the family sat down to have breakfast. "We'll find out what's bothering the little girl."

"Mom, may I please go with you?" begged Billy.

"I don't think that's a good idea, Billy," she replied. "School just started, and you shouldn't take a day off."

"Please, Mom?"

After some deliberation, Cathy rethought her decision and told Billy that he could accompany them. Dan agreed that it might be a good idea: another learning experience.

⚜

On leash, Lady dutifully followed Cathy and Billy into the vet's office. After checking in, they sat and waited for an examination room to become available. They entered and waited anxiously for the vet.

"What seems to be the problem?" the vet asked.

"She's not been eating, even her favorite things," Billy offered.

"And she's been drinking a lot of water," Cathy said. "It all started the day after her eighth birthday party, on Saturday. She ate a good meal that evening: rice, hamburger, green beans and carrots with some cottage cheese mixed in. She loves that stuff. It's nothing serious, is it, doctor?"

"Billy, Cathy, it might be a good idea to take a wellness test. That means a blood sample and urine sample that will be sent to the lab for analysis. The test would check her vital organs to see how they're operating and it will issue a report on the values. Do you think you could get Lady to provide a urine sample outside?"

"I can try," volunteered Billy as Cathy nodded in agreement. "Let's try," she said.

Mother and son took Lady outside onto the grounds of the Sunnyside Animal Hospital. As she squatted to pee, Cathy placed the capture cup under her. When Lady finished, they took the cup back into the office and handed it to the receptionist and returned to the exam room.

The vet returned, took Lady into another room for a blood sample, and returned her to the exam room. "We'll have the results in a day or two," he offered. "I prefer to send the samples out for analysis. The lab provides a far more accurate report than we can provide here. Please give the office a call tomorrow afternoon. They should be back by two."

"Thanks, doctor," a seemingly far more mature Billy said. "We'll do that."

❦

Fingers trembling, Cathy dialed the vet's office the following afternoon. She had refused Billy's request to take a second day off from school. She decided to tackle the issue on her own.

"Sunnyside Animal Hospital," the voice on the other end said.

"Hello, this is Mrs. Cooper, calling regarding the tests taken on Foxy Lady yesterday. Have the results come in yet?" she asked.

"One moment please, Mrs. Cooper."

In under a minute the receptionist returned to the phone. "Mrs. Cooper, the doctor asked if you could stop by."

Fear took hold of Cathy as she replied that she would be there as soon as possible.

"Mrs. Cooper, I'm sorry," the vet said after she arrived. "It appears to be renal failure. It's a condition that is not uncommon in the fox terrier breed, although it's not necessarily so common at so young an age."

"Oh good heavens!" Cathy exclaimed. "Can anything be done for her?"

"What bothers me most is that she's not been eating," said the vet. "With kidney disease, that is a sign. Lady is losing protein via her urine."

Cathy asked, "If that's the case, could we increase her protein intake, so that the amount lost can be replaced?"

"No," the vet replied. "It's not that simple. The more protein that she's given, the harder it is for her kidneys to process it. I can put her on a prescription diet that controls the amount of protein that she gets, if she'll eat it. It's a diet that is especially prepared for canines suffering from kidney failure."

"Whatever you say, doctor," Cathy said in a voice that trembled. "Billy so loves Lady … all of us love her. Please do whatever you feel is best. Is there any hope for her?"

"We've had success, in the past, with being able to prolong the life of dogs in renal failure for anywhere from a few weeks for up to two years," he replied. "It all depends on the degree of failure. From what the tests reveal, Lady is approaching an advanced stage of kidney failure. I'm so sorry, Mrs. Cooper."

Biting her lower lip, Cathy said, "Please, please do whatever you feel might help. Billy will be devastated!"

"The first thing that I'd suggest is that she be given fluids, every other day. This can be done at home, or if you prefer, here at the office. We'll show you how it's done."

The vet's assistant, Kaitlin, gently pinched Lady at the nape of her neck and created a "tent." Into that tent she inserted a needle. Then she grasped a bag of fluid, squeezing it to begin the flow that would force it into Lady. A "bubble" appeared at the site where the fluid entered. There appeared to be no pain or discomfort, but it was a professional that was providing the service. Cathy wasn't certain that she or Dan, much less Billy, would be able to administer the fluid without causing pain or injury to Lady.

"Doctor," she asked, "Would it be possible for me or Dan to bring Lady into the office to have this procedure done? I honestly don't know if any of us would be capable of doing it at home without hurting Lady."

"We can make arrangements for 'nursing service,' and you could bring her into the office for the treatment," the vet replied. "As you've noted, it only takes a few minutes. It's also vital that you get her to eat. At this point, anything."

Before leaving, the receptionist produced a twelve-pack case of prescription canned dog food along with a bag of prescription dry food. An aide took the food to Cathy's car and they returned home.

❦

Dinnertime came and went. Lady walked to her food dish, took a quick sniff, and walked off without taking as much as a bite. Neither the moist, canned food nor the dry pellets could entice her to eat.

Cathy boiled some chicken breast, adding only a dash of garlic powder for added flavor. After it cooled, she shredded it and replaced the food dish with the chicken. Normally Lady would eat chicken breast in a heartbeat. Again, she sniffed at it and walked away.

"Ummmmmmmm, this is good," said Billy the next day at breakfast as he offered Lady a small portion of scrambled egg whites. She looked at him, cocked her head (as dogs so often do), sniffed the dish, and slowly walked off, uninterested.

So it went the remainder of the day. All attempts to coerce Lady to eat failed, although she continued to drink water in amounts greater than normal.

Dan arrived home from work. He entered the kitchen carrying a six-pack of vanilla-flavored nutritional drinks, rationalizing that the supplement with its two dozen or so essential vitamins and minerals might spark her appetite. It was no go. Lady sniffed and sauntered onto the lanai.

She remained somewhat playful, but she did not initiate playtime, responding to Billy's ball-tossing halfheartedly, but losing interest far more quickly than normally.

The entire Cooper family felt depression setting in on them as they continued to look for signs, hoping that Lady's lack of appetite was only temporary. Cathy jotted down notes that she would take with her to the vet the following day for her "irrigation" treatment, as Cathy referred to it.

Many prayers were directed heavenward as each family member pleaded with an unseen God to intervene in Lady's behalf.

Except for Lady, who slept soundly and peacefully through the night, sleep did not come easily for any of the other Coopers.

CHAPTER 10

Treatments Continue

The vet listened attentively as Cathy read off her laundry list of observations, all the various foods they attempted to get Lady to eat.

"And she didn't eat any of that at all?" he asked.

"Nothing substantial. One day she might pick here and there, and the next day she'd turn up her nose at the very thing she seemed to enjoy the day before. Dan even tried to offer a vitamin/mineral nutritional shake. It smelled good. She wouldn't touch it. I actually finished the remains of the six-ounce bottle, and it was delicious," Cathy replied. "But she does drink more water than usual."

"That's fairly typical in cases of kidney failure, especially in advanced failure," the vet said. "If you like, we can give her a shot of anti-nausea medication. Normally it's quite painful, but if we inject into the fluid's 'bubble,' she won't feel a thing. It might help to stimulate her appetite."

"Of course, please do," Cathy replied. "Anything to get her appetite back."

Lady's body accepted the fluid treatment quite readily, indicating that her body needed the liquid. As the vet had indicated, there was not a flicker of pain when the anti-nausea shot was administered.

Cathy and Lady returned home.

It was Friday, and Lady would not be returning to the vet's until Monday for her next treatment.

That weekend, the Coopers once again tried everything to get her to eat. Each member of the family came up with possible solutions. Dan suggested a medium-rare New York strip steak. It worked; however, Lady only took a few nibbles, then she walked away. She was showing signs of distancing herself more and more each day, something that dogs do when they're not feeling well. Unlike humans, who seek attention and complain about their symptoms, dogs never complain. Instead they tend to withdraw, preferring to be alone, perhaps in an attempt not to disappoint their human friends.

It appears that animals display a good deal more intelligence than humans. A dog wishes to please its master. Few people like complainers. Humans might learn a few things from their animal friends.

Lady was slowing down. Surely the lack of food/fuel in her body would cause that. Cathy made a mental note to check her weight on each subsequent visit to the vet.

The Cooper household was a somber place all weekend as everyone once again tried to think of something that would return Lady's appetite. From fish to vegetables (she loved carrots and green beans) to puppy ice cream, to puddings, fast-food burgers, nothing could convince Lady that she should eat.

"I can't think of anything that we haven't tried," a troubled Dan said. "Can anyone?"

"How about a pizzeria pizza?" Billy asked. "Maybe the smell of the spices would help perk her up!"

"It's certainly worth a try," Cathy added. "I'll go and pick one up. Want to join me, Billy?"

"I'll stay here, Mom, with Lady, if you don't mind."

Lady had always loved to go for a ride in the car, so Cathy replied, "How about if we take Lady with us? You know how she enjoys riding in the car, being a back-seat driver. How about it?"

"Sure," quipped Billy. "Lady, wanna go for a ride in the car?"

Lady's ears perked up as she headed toward the laundry room that led to the garage.

"Atta girl!" shouted Billy. "Let's go!"

Lady jumped into the front seat of the car, then assumed her normal position with her back legs on the back seat and her front paws on the console between the seats, barking all the while. This was her element … riding in the car with those she loved and barking her approval of the progress of the ride, but mostly barking at oncoming motorcycles. Oh how she hated those bikes and how she loved barking at them!

A half-hour later they returned, pizza in hand. As they entered the kitchen from the laundry room, Billy said, "Lady, take a whiff of this," as he extended the box containing the pizza toward her.

She took a sniff then followed Billy as he placed the box on the island in the kitchen and proceeded to open it.

Carefully searching for any signs of hot pepper flakes (which they told the server they did not want on the pizza), Billy cut off the hard outer crust and broke the remainder into small, bite-sized pieces and placed them into Lady's dish. She sniffed, then walked to her water dish and took several laps of water ... then she returned to the food dish and promptly emptied it!

When offered a second portion, however, she dismissed it and walked onto the lanai. After she looked at the glistening water in the pool for a few minutes, she plopped down at the pool's edge, closed her eyes and took a nap.

The entire family was elated that she'd eaten. She might want more later on, so the remaining pizza was carefully covered with wax paper, the box closed and kept on the island bar so it would retain its freshness rather than lose some by refrigerating it.

When "later on" arrived, she would have no part of a second serving of pizza ... only water. The happiness that the family felt earlier had been cancelled out by the moment.

They kept a keen watch on her for the remainder of the day.

❧

Monday came and after Billy left for school, Cathy busied herself by clearing the few breakfast dishes, rinsing them and placing them into the dishwasher. She poured a third cup of coffee for herself. There was still time before she and Lady were expected at the vet. As she sat down to her coffee, she made an impromptu list of the additional foods they'd tried since Friday's visit to show to the vet. It looked like a grocery list that she'd normally prepare for the weekly visit to the supermarket. Was there anything they'd not tried?

"This is obviously not working as I had hoped," the vet admitted as he scanned the list of foods the Coopers had tried over the weekend. He then suggested medication for the disease itself, to be taken twice daily. He explained to Cathy that the medicine could hasten the deterioration; however it could restore some quality of life for Lady in the process. In addition to the twice-daily medication, Lady would be given an anti-nausea shot every other day.

He gave Cathy instructions on administering the capsules, one in the morning and one before dinner-time. "Take a small dollop of creamy peanut butter on your fingertip and encase the capsule in it. Open her mouth by holding her snout just enough to be able to insert your finger part of the way. Push your finger up to the roof of her mouth, then with it in that position, remove your finger. Just be watchful that she doesn't spit it out," he cautioned.

"I will," Cathy said as her heart ached for the little terrier who had brought so much love and joy to the household—to everyone, not only Billy. "Oh, doctor, I almost forgot," Cathy added, "would it be possible to weigh her?"

"Of course," the vet replied. "First let's have Gretchen and Kaitlin administer her fluids, then we can take Lady off the exam table and lower it. The table doubles as a scale."

Lady's body accepted the fluid readily. She was in a state of dehydration, and the sac that the fluid produced disappeared almost immediately.

After the treatment, Cathy learned that Lady weighed in at 21.2 pounds, just about 0.8 shy of her normal weight of 22.0 lbs.

Cathy scrawled the number down in a small note-book that she always carried in her purse, adding the date. She made a mental note to keep a running log of Lady's weight along with the date.

CHAPTER 11

Treatments Are Failing

For three weeks, Cathy took Lady to the vet three days a week for her hydration treatments. In those three weeks, the terrier's weight fluctuated, going down to as low as 19.6 pounds. One day her weight would be down a fraction of a pound, and the days after she ate, it would go up several tenths of a pound. Overall, however, she was losing weight.

On their final visit for the week, Lady weighed 19.8 pounds. She still displayed signs of interest in playing, on her terms, when she felt that she wanted to play and only for as long as she felt up to playing. It was heart rending to watch Lady deteriorate and be powerless to help her..

"Mrs. Cooper, I think we should change Lady's schedule and provide the fluid on a daily basis from now on," suggested the vet. "That would include Saturdays. Our office is open Saturdays from 8:00 a.m. to 12:30 p.m. Would this work for you?"

"Yes," replied Cathy, clearly despondent and disappointed over the failure of past treatments and medicines to bring Lady around. "What time would you like me to stop by tomorrow?" she added.

"It would be fine if you stopped in around 11:30," he responded, "Business is usually slow for the last hour; however, if an emergency comes in you may need to wait."

"Of course, I understand. Thank you, I'll see you then." Cathy left, Lady trailing behind her.

Lady no longer appeared to want to be the leader. She was clearly failing. All of the good intentions and medical advances failed to provide the desired results.

❧

"It's not working, Billy. Lady isn't responding positively to the treatments and medicine," Cathy told her son when he returned from school. "Her weight is down to 19.8 pounds. That's a loss of 2.2 pounds in barely three weeks. That's unacceptable for a dog her size."

"Mom, she isn't going to die, is she?" Billy asked, obviously in turmoil from the news. He turned to wipe his eyes as they began to well up with tears.

"Honey, I don't know. I just don't know. Starting tomorrow I'll be taking her for treatments six days a week. You're welcome to come with me, if you feel that you'd be up to it."

Dan and Cathy had made it a point to be totally honest not only with each other, but also with their son.

"Sure, I want to go along," Billy replied. "Let's see if we can find something that she'll eat."

Billy opened a can of soup: chicken with egg noodles and carrots. He carefully picked out the small chunks of chicken along with the carrots and placed them in a small dish rather than Lady's normal food dish. The chicken, protein, was not good for Lady in her condition, yet the vet had indicated that she must eat, and as he had said, "At this point, anything."

Lady slowly walked to the dish and sniffed. She took a few laps of water from the water bowl then returned to the smaller dish and began eating. She ate slowly as if her heart were not really in it, but she managed to consume the three or four ounces that it contained.

Billy poured the remainder into another dish and heated it in the microwave. He'd share the soup with Lady. She wasn't fond of noodles but they wouldn't go to waste.

"Mom, would you like some chicken soup?" he asked Cathy. "If you would, I could pick out the carrots and chicken for Lady and you could have the rest."

"Sure, dear," Cathy responded, although she really wasn't hungry. "If Lady eats more, that would be wonderful!"

As he opened the second can and spooned out Lady's portion, he glanced down toward Lady. She was lying down on a carpet in front of the refrigerator. Instead of standing at his side in anticipation of a treat of chicken and carrots, she displayed no interest in what he was doing. She did eat almost half of the second small helping. It appeared that she was trying to please her "family" rather than satisfy the hunger pangs that she suffered yet ignored due to the nausea caused by her disease. Dogs are known to want to please their owners.

Cathy and Billy glanced toward the laundry room door as they heard the garage door being opened. Dan was home from work. As he entered the kitchen, it was obvious by the look on their faces that all was not well.

"What's the news?" Dan asked, knowing that his question would cause more pain for his wife and son.

Cathy related the results of their visit to the vet, explaining that starting next week, Lady's treatment would become daily, six days a week.

"She did eat a bit of chicken and carrots from canned chicken soup earlier," Cathy offered. "Not a lot, but considering how poorly she's been eating since this condition developed, I'm somewhat pleased with her intake, but she only weighed 19.8 today."

❦

Sunday morning the phone rang, shattering the silence of the extraordinarily hot day.

"It's Grandma," Billy announced.

"Mom, thanks for calling. How are you and Dad?" Cathy asked. She smiled slightly as her mother replied that they were both well. She was calling to learn how Lady was doing. "Not well at all, Mom. She's lost weight and she merely picks at food most of the time, if she eats at all. But for the most part she just walks away from her dish and lies down, preferring to be alone." They chatted for a few minutes about life in general. Then the call was ended as Cathy said into the phone, "I love you too, Mom. Thanks so much for calling, and please give Dad a hug and kiss for us. Bye!"

It was very quiet in the Cooper house for the remainder of the day, with the loudest sound being the occasional rustle of paper as Dan read the Sunday newspaper and the snip of scissors as Cathy clipped coupons in preparation of her next visit to the supermarket.

Billy tried to stay close to Lady, lying on a towel on the lanai. But Lady, as much as she wanted to please her best friend, didn't want company. Each time he edged close to her, she'd get up and distance herself from him just a few inches. Not far, just enough to satisfy herself that she was "alone."

Indeed, all was not nearly well in the Cooper household. It was a long, long Sunday as petitions for Lady's welfare continued to be sent heavenward.

CHAPTER 12

Facing the Inevitable

Lady was voted Pet of the Month by the veterinarian staff that month. It was an honor bestowed on the staff members' "favorite" pet, and in the past few months every staff member at the veterinary hospital had the opportunity to meet and treat Lady.

Another two weeks had passed. It seemed that Lady would only eat every other day as dictated by her hunger pangs, and very sparingly at that. Her water consumption increased. She began "making mistakes" in the house as a result.

The last weigh-in showed her at 16.2 pounds, 3.6 pounds less than the 19.8 pounds that she weighed a few weeks earlier. Clearly she was failing, yet she displayed no outward signs of pain; she continued to give as much love to her family as her deterioration would permit.

The family, likewise, was showering her with love, but Dan, Cathy, and Billy were all clearly in despair at being helpless to do anything that would truly benefit her. Nobody wanted to be the one to bring up the subject of the inevitable, certainly not Billy. Dan felt that it had to be discussed, and soon. He would wait until he got the report after the next visit to the vet. That was tomorrow.

A fatigued Cathy led the way into the kitchen, followed by a moping Foxy Lady. Still, the valiant Lady failed to display any outward signs of illness or pain.

After Billy returned from school, Cathy filled him in regarding the latest results. Understandably, he was very upset.

"Mom, I'm really afraid," he said, his eyes filling with tears.

"Dear, I think we need to face the fact that Lady isn't going to improve. I think it's time for us as a family to make a decision. We need to 'let go' and release Lady," Cathy said, also crying. "Think about it. It's selfish to keep her alive when there is no quality to that life and no hope of improving. She's not enjoying herself as she had been until a few months ago. We merely serve 'our' desires by trying to keep her alive when she's ready to be released, Billy."

"Son," she added, "Animals know when it's time to go. I think that Lady might be trying to tell us that it's getting close to her time. She's a brave little girl. She's doing as much as she can in order to please us, but she's overwhelmed. She has no appetite. As a result she's losing weight and she's getting weaker by the day. It's getting more and more difficult for her to please us. She realizes that pleasing her family is her 'job,' but she's no longer capable of doing it.

"Elephants might be a good example of this. They're considered to be among the more intelligent creatures in the animal kingdom. Elephants seem to know when it's time for them to die. To survive they need to eat lots of vegetation over the course of their lifetime. The constant chewing wears their teeth down. In their lifetime they grow up to four sets of teeth, but at some point in time their last set wears down and they can no longer chew the massive amounts of vegetation that they need to survive. They know when it's time for them to die, and if they're able to, they will travel across many miles to go to the 'elephant graveyard' where they actually starve to death."

Cathy could see that Billy clearly understood the comparison of the elephant story in his mind. But in his heart, he was not prepared to accept it.

Dan returned home from work and entered the kitchen, giving Cathy a kiss as he tousled Billy's hair. "How's it going, Sport?" he asked.

"Not good, Dad. Mom was just explaining how elephants die, and how they know when it's time. But I know that she was really talking about Lady," the boy replied.

Amazed, Cathy cupped her hands under Billy's chin and lovingly kissed the top of the boy's head.

"It's gotten to the point that I had to, Dan," Cathy said.

"Cathy, I'm so proud of you for taking the initiative," said Dan. "I was preparing myself to have the same discussion as I walked in the door. Billy, I'm proud of you too, for understanding. In fact, I don't think that I could be any prouder of you than I am at this moment."

"Dad, Mom, I know that it's the right decision to make, but my heart is breaking," Billy sobbed.

They all hugged as they looked at the weary Lady who was lying on the floor facing a corner as if she were being punished. It's something that dogs are known to do when they're not feeling well.

The first thing tomorrow they would call the vet and arrange for what needed to be done.

CHAPTER 13

Letting Go

Saturday, Dan was off and Lady was due at the vet's for her treatment at 11:30. Dan didn't wait. Lady was in too much distress at that point. He dialed the vet's office. When the receptionist answered, he said, "This is Dan Cooper calling. Lady appears to be in pain. She's lethargic and she's distanced herself from the rest of the family. It's really painful to see her suffering. We have all come to realize that it's time to 'let go.'"

"I'm so sorry, Mr. Cooper," the voice replied. "We have a procedure scheduled for 9:45, but we can make arrangements to attend to Lady at 8:45 if that is suitable for your family."

Dan related the message to Cathy and Billy. Both responded with a reluctant silent nod as they glanced in Lady's direction.

"Thank you, we'll be there," Dan replied.

Billy sat on the floor facing the same corner Lady was facing, gently petting her. He didn't attempt to offer her anything to eat, but he did place her water dish nearby. Occasionally she turned and took a few laps.

Cathy carefully took Lady's favorite blanket from the doggie bed that Lady hadn't used in so long and folded it to take along to the vet's.

Dan sipped on a cup of coffee, wasting time until it was time to leave. At 8:30 they went to the car, a leashed Lady trailing the pack with a slower-than-ever gait. Normally she'd be the first in the car, but she had to be helped in this morning. Billy sat in the back, holding Lady partly on his lap. She wasn't interested in assuming her normal position, front feet on the console, back feet on the rear seat. Nothing was the same. Soon, nothing would be the same ever again.

CHAPTER 14

A Final Goodbye

"Good morning," the receptionist said, realizing as she said it, that it was hardly a "good" morning, when the family entered the waiting room. "I'm so sorry."

The trio merely nodded a greeting. Billy was holding Lady in his arms, atop her favorite blanket.

Kaitlin and Gretchen appeared from one of the treatment rooms. Kaitlin approached Lady, kissed her gently on the nose, and said, "Hi, sweet baby ... oh, you're such a sweet little girl, aren't you? Yes, you are!"

There was no response from Lady; her eyes were partially closed.

"Could you please follow me," Gretchen said, leading the way into the second treatment room. "We'll prepare Lady here. If you want to stay with her, you're welcome to. We'll be inserting a catheter into her left front leg after shaving it."

The trio elected to go to the waiting room. It was too much to bear.

"That's fine," said Gretchen. "I'll let you know when we're ready."

Several minutes later, Gretchen appeared in the doorway and beckoned the Coopers. "We're ready," she said.

Kaitlin was gently petting Lady, who was still lying on her favorite blanket. She was now too weak to stand for any great length of time.

"Sweet baby," Kaitlin kept repeating.

The vet entered from an anteroom, holding two small vials.

Positioning himself at one side of the table he nodded, purposely avoiding a "good morning," considering that there was nothing good about it for the Coopers.

"This vial contains a sedative. It will simply put Lady into a sleep state. There will be absolutely no pain or discomfort. And this one," he said, exposing the second vial, "will complete the action."

The Coopers each had a hand on Lady: Cathy on her head, Billy under her chin, and Dan gently stroking her back. Their grief was extreme. Tears filled their eyes. Gretchen and Kaitlin also sniffed, wiping their eyes with a tissue as Gretchen handed a small wad of tissues to each of the Coopers.

"Do you want a few minutes to say your goodbyes?" the vet asked.

Dan and Cathy shook their heads, indicating a "no." They were as ready as they could possibly be. They couldn't bear to allow Lady to suffer any longer than necessary.

Kissing Lady gently, first on her forehead, then on her nose, Billy said, "My little Lady. I love you so much, my little friend. Soon all of your pain will be gone. I promise you."

The vet administered the first shot. Lady's head gently lowered in Billy's hand. Her breathing slowed, remaining steady.

Carefully inserting the second needled into the catheter, the fluid entered Lady's vein. In less than two seconds it was done. The doctor placed his stethoscope to her heart, repositioned it several times and said, "It's over, she's gone."

After giving the grieving family time to absorb what had just taken place, yet respecting their private moments after Lady's death, Gretchen and Kaitlin, who had remained with the family after the doctor left, initiated a group embrace. Gretchen was the first to speak.

"I am so, so sorry. Have you thought about how you wanted to handle Lady's remains?" she asked.

Dan spoke for the family. "I think that we'd like to have her cremated," he said, "so that her remains can still be a part of our lives."

Billy, still in tears, whispered, "Dad, you didn't have either Sadie or Cosmo cremated. Why Lady?"

Dan explained that pet cremation wasn't an option at the time those dogs passed, but times had changed and many pet owners now opted for cremation.

"Is there anything that Sunnyside Animal Hospital can do to assist you?" Gretchen asked.

"No, thank you," Dan replied. "We'll take care of the rest. If you could call the crematorium and let them know that we're on our way, I'd appreciate it."

"I'm so very sorry," both Kaitlin and Gretchen said in unison as each gave Lady a farewell kiss as they gently stroked her now-still body, a body that was finally released from pain.

"I'll be sure to call them," Gretchen added. "Do you have the address?"

Dan nodded affirmatively.

Dan noted, and would later mention to Cathy and Billy, that the two girls had genuinely bonded with Lady over the course of her treatments. Their care and concern far surpassed professionalism. They truly grew to love their precious little girl. Dan surprised Cathy and Billy as he uttered a barely audible prayer thanking God for the time that He had permitted Lady to be a part of their lives, adding "We wish that Your will had been to allow her more time with us."

The prayer was most unusual since for most of his life Dan found it difficult to believe in God, at least a god who heard prayers and acted on them. It appeared that he was "growing" in his attitude toward religion.

Cathy and Billy added "Amen," along with Dan.

After a few final minutes with their friend, Dan picked up the limp body, being careful not to cover it (she was part of the family—to cover her, to "hide" her would be to deny her existence), he took her to the car and placed her lovingly on the back seat. Billy joined her, gently stroking the lifeless body all the way to the crematorium.

※

Dan was greeted at the crematorium by one of its employees who had stepped outside for a cigarette break. "Mr. Cooper?" he asked.

"Yes," Dan said, adding, "With Lady."

"Please follow me," the man said after crunching his cigarette into a sand-filled coffee can that stood outside the door.

The family followed as Dan carefully removed Lady from the car.

"What a sweet-looking dog," the worker said. They proceeded into the crematorium. As instructed, Dan placed Lady's remains onto a stainless steel table, blanket intact under her, and told the worker that the family wanted Lady cremated alone, not as part of a group cremation, with other animals.

The worker replied that all private cremations are done with only the one animal, as he placed Lady into a metal container and placed her into the facility, closed the door and turned the controls on.

"Folks," the man added, "Our cremations are done with the utmost of respect, just a cremations for a human are done. We understand your loss and we treat your 'family member' as we would want one of our own family treated."

Based on Lady's weight, the procedure would take about ninety minutes. Dan was told that he could pick up the cremains later that day (they would be open until 2:00 p.m.) or on Monday. Dan chose the former, stating that he'd return before two. They left the crematorium procedure room.

Together, the family chose a simple two-toned wooden box, much like a jewelry box, to house Lady's cremains. It would bear her date of birth and death on a metal plate that would be placed on the top of the small casket like container.

CHAPTER 15

Life Goes On

Several days after Foxy Lady's death, a card appeared among a small handful of bills and circulars in the morning mail. The return address showed that it came from Sunnyside Animal Hospital. The inside of the sympathy card bore a short personal note and the signature of each employee, including the vet's.

A smaller card, much like a prayer card, was tucked inside the larger card. It contained a beautiful poem that read:

The Rainbow Bridge

Just this side of heaven is a place called Rainbow Bridge. When an animal dies that has been especially close to someone here, that pet goes to Rainbow Bridge. There are meadows and hills for all of our special friends so they can run and play together. There is plenty of food, water, and sunshine, and our friends are warm and comfortable.

All the animals who had been ill and old are restored to health and vigor. Those who were hurt or maimed are made whole and strong again, just as we remember them in our dreams of days and times gone by. The animals are happy and content, except for one small thing; they each miss someone very special to them, who had to be left behind.

They all run and play together, but the day comes when one suddenly stops and looks into the distance. His bright eyes are intent. His eager body quivers. Suddenly he begins to run from the group, flying over the green grass, his legs carrying him faster and faster.

You have been spotted, and when you and your special friend finally meet, you cling together in joyous reunion, never to be parted again. The happy kisses rain upon your face; your hands again caress the beloved head, and you look once more into the trusting eyes of your pet, so long gone from your life but never absent from your heart.

Then you cross Rainbow Bridge together ...

Author unknown

"How lovely," Cathy said as a few tears welled in her eyes as she reread the touching poem.

Dan and Billy agreed after reading the small card. "I wish that were true," Billy said, also in tears.

Dan replied, "Me, too. Lady is the third dog that I've lost in my lifetime. It would be wonderful to be able to believe that someday I'd be with them again, but I have never been one to believe in fairy tales. Perhaps the day will come when I can.

For days after Lady's death, Dan, Cathy, and Billy all experienced similar emotions: hearing the familiar jingle of her chain collar or the sound of a rubber ball bouncing along the tiled areas of the floors, even hearing the "slurp, slurp" of Lady taking a few laps of water.

Slowly life for the Coopers began to return to normal, although each time they passed the wooden box on the mantel or merely looked in that direction, each felt a pang of pain for their fallen companion. Yet, the thought of moving the box elsewhere, somewhere out of sight, never became an issue. To ignore Lady would be to deny her existence and every last bit of happiness that she brought into their lives, and they into hers. So they looked at it often, and with pride. Eventually it brought some consolation.

Billy resumed his after-school activities of swimming and diving. It was difficult at first, but he found it was a bit less difficult to cope with his loss if his mind were distracted.

His coach had honored Dan's request to temporarily suspend the practice pending the outcome of their ordeal. Several weeks later, Billy was able to concentrate on his talents for swimming and diving without constantly thinking of Lady, but he seemed to be rebelling, "paying God back" for having taken his beloved friend from him. He dismissed cautionary rules of conduct both on the diving boards and in the pool.

The coach had high hopes for Billy. He was an extremely talented young man, yet he felt the need to admonish the boy for his recent conduct and somewhat negative attitude.

Although he apologized to the coach, Billy's attitude did not indicate a serious change of heart.

CHAPTER 16

Disaster Strikes Again

It was late morning on a crisp fall day more than a year later when the phone rang. It was the guidance counselor from Billy's school. "Mrs. Cooper? This is Miss Jennings, Billy's guidance counselor calling. I'm afraid that there's been an accident and Billy's been taken to the hospital."

Cutting the woman short as a lump formed in her throat, Cathy asked, "What? What accident? How is he?"

"Mrs. Cooper, I've already called Mr. Cooper at work. He's on his way to pick you up. He didn't want you to drive."

"But, but how is he?" Cathy repeated.

"I'm terribly sorry, Mrs. Cooper. The hospital would not provide any information to me since I'm not a member of the immediate family."

Cathy hung up the phone, feeling weak in her knees she could feel her stomach suddenly get knotted. She almost passed out as Dan walked in the door.

Hugging Cathy and giving her a kiss on her forehead, Dan said, "Cath, they wouldn't tell me anything on the phone. Are you ready to leave?"

She'd been in the midst of cleaning when the call came in. She went into the bathroom, looked in the mirror, splashed some cold water on her face and patted it dry. She brushed her hair back with her hand and said, "Yes, please hurry!"

☙❧

Billy was connected to a life-support system when they rushed into his hospital room. A nurse was also in the room monitoring the equipment and jotting down notes on a chart.

"Oh, my God! Billy, oh Billy!" cried a distraught Cathy, as Dan stood behind her, looking at the machine his son was attached to. "God in heaven, what did we do to deserve this?"

The nurse didn't speak, permitting the couple to release their pent-up emotions as she continued to monitor the controls on the system.

At that moment, two neurologists entered the room, took Billy's chart from the nurse, and stood, studying it.

"What happened?" Cathy asked again. "Nobody has told us anything!"

"Mr. Cooper, Mrs. Cooper," replied one of the doctors at Billy's bedside, "we understand that there was bit of horseplay at swimming practice, and your son slipped on the wet surface surrounding the pool and hit his head on one of the ladders. He is in a coma with brain injuries. His brain has swelled. The next twenty-four hours will be crucial to his recovery."

"Oh, my God," screamed Cathy. "Oh, my dear God!

"We have taken a series of tests," the doctor offered. "Little can be done to reverse any injuries. We're doing everything that we can to insure a proper blood flow to Billy's brain. He has not been responding as we had hoped."

"What more can be done?" asked a frantic Dan.

"All that we can do at this time, Mr. Cooper, is monitor his progress and hope that he will show some response to treatment," the doctor replied. "We have taken all the precautions and steps that modern science has to offer. A coma involves two different concepts: reactivity and perceptivity. A person in a coma does not experience reactivity or perceptivity. The person cannot be aroused by calling their name or by experiencing pain."

"Doctor, please explain in terms that an ordinary person can understand," a distraught Dan demanded.

"Mr. Cooper, Mrs. Cooper," the doctor continued, "Billy's condition appears to be very bleak: not at all hopeful."

"Oh, my God in heaven," Cathy cried. "Are you saying that our son is going to die?"

"I am so sorry, Mrs. Cooper, but his condition is not promising," the doctor replied. "His injury was extremely severe and he has not been responding to treatment. The intracranial pressure appears to be increasing. The prognosis is not good. We're attempting to control that pressure with intensive monitoring and control of all bodily functions. This will require attention around the clock. His breathing is being controlled by a ventilator, and he's been given medications to temporarily paralyze him. This needs to be done to control his breathing, blood pressure, and other vital bodily functions. He has not responded to treatment and all signs indicate brain death."

The second neurologist, not speaking, nodded in agreement.

Cathy and Dan stared at their son in disbelief. This could not be happening. What had they done, or failed to do in their lives for a loving God to place this burden upon them? Precisely what had they done?

Not wanting to risk further injury to his head with even the most gentle of kisses, each parent lovingly placed a hand on one of Billy's hands, which were resting on his chest.

"Brain death?" asked Cathy, simultaneously with Dan. "Just what does that mean?" Cathy pleaded.

"Brain death," explained the neurologist, "is an irreversible end of all brain activity, including the involuntary activity that is necessary to sustain life. It is due to the necrosis of cerebral neurons following loss of oxygen to the brain. Brain death in either the entire brain or in the brain stem is a legal indicator of death."

"You're saying that Billy *is* dead?" Dan asked.

"In medical and legal definitions, yes," the neurologist replied as his associate nodded in agreement. "There has been absolutely no response to any treatment," he repeated.

"Of course, you're more than welcome to call in a neurologist of your choice for another opinion." It was the first time the second doctor had spoken.

Releasing Billy's hand, Cathy collapsed onto a chair at his bedside, burying her face in her own hands as the tears began to flow with no sign of stopping.

Dan also released his hand from Billy's, bent over to kiss the boy ever so lightly, then knelt at his wife's side, attempting to console her even though he was also in desperate need of consolation.

"He's gone. Our son is gone," said an inconsolable Cathy. "Why?" she shouted, looking heavenward. "Why?"

"There is no answer to that 'why,'" the first neurologist offered. "Sometimes there is simply no answer to what life throws our way."

"What now?" asked Dan. "What is the next step?"

"We recommend that Billy remain on life-support for a period of twenty-four hours," the doctor replied. "If there is no change, no improvement in that time, the next step would be to disconnect the life-support system."

Neither parent was able to fathom that thought. Life was so cruel—too cruel. Parents should not outlive their children. That's not how life is meant to be.

"I hesitate to mention this," the neurologist said, "but you might want to think about Billy becoming an organ donor. You might want to discuss it in the upcoming hours in the event there is no substantial change in his condition."

"No! That's going too far! I can barely think at this time," Dan said. "And you're ready to dissect our son and distribute his 'parts' to other people? I simply will not even consider that 'option.'"

"I understand," the doctor said, leaving the nurse to her duties and the Coopers to their grief. The second doctor followed closely behind.

❧

Dan and Cathy remained at the hospital that night. Neither ate a bite, surviving on coffee after coffee from a machine in the hallway. They barely spoke. The only sounds in the room were the "beep-beep" of the life-support system, a monotonous reminder of the life it was working to save—unsuccessfully—and the rustle of the night-shift nurse's dress as she moved from control to control, carefully recording each reading on her chart.

Finally Cathy broke the silence. "Dan," she said, "About that donor thing that the doctor mentioned, I've been thinking about that. If worse comes to worst, Billy could continue to live on in someone else. His gift of life could possibly save other lives; help other desperate parents to cope. That could be a testimony to the zest that he had for life as well as his unselfishness. It's a decision we might want to rethink. I know that I'd look for such an option if one were offered to us."

Dan nodded. "If that is something that you feel you want to do, we can make that determination if and when the time comes. There is still hope Cath. Don't you agree?"

Cathy kissed him gently in reply. *Yes, there must be hope*, she thought to herself. *I'll never give that up.*

Finally a troubled sleep came to them in short bursts as each sat in a chair at Billy's bedside, sleep interrupted only by brief strange dreams, all involving various facets of Billy's life.

The night dragged by, the beep-beep of the life-support keeping track of time—the precious little time that remained.

Daylight came with a furious tropical depression casting rain on the hospital room windows, the continuous sound competing for attention with the beep-beep of the life-support machine.

At about 9:30 a.m., the two neurologists entered the room. Glancing at the shift nurses' notes from throughout the day and night, and checking the controls on the machine, the doctors' thoughts could be read by the sideways motion of their heads. Nothing had changed.

Both Dan and Cathy noticed that movement as their hearts sunk lower than they thought possible.

"We're so sorry," the first doctor said, taking Cathy's hand as the second doctor placed what was meant to be a reassuring hand on Dan's shoulder. "There has been no change."

"You're saying," Dan replied, "that it's all over? That Billy is dead?"

"Brain-dead," replied the first doctor. "He is legally dead although the life-support machine continues to breathe for him and continues to keep his vital organs functioning."

Cathy didn't utter a word. Her grief was unbearable; she was incapable of talking. Billy's life, from the moment of birth to this very moment, flashed before her, in a montage of events that included bumps and kisses on an injured knee, his first day of school, Lady's passing and so much more.

Dan and Cathy were asked to sign the necessary papers that permitted the doctors to remove the life-support system.

Each in turn signed the forms with quivering hands. Cathy handed the paperwork to the neurologist who once again took her hand, then took Dan's hand in a gentle handshake and repeated, "I am so sorry." He then left the room.

The second doctor explained that after the equipment was turned off, it could take anywhere from several minutes to nearly an hour for all bodily functions to cease. He then disabled the machine and stood to the side.

Each parent kissed the boy's face and head, again and again, realizing that there was no further risk of injury, no chance of causing pain. "Goodbye, Billy, my beloved son," Cathy said.

Dan stood beside her, tears streaming down his face, as he said a mental farewell to his son, *goodbye, dear son.*

The beep-beep of the machine stopped. The visual monitor was the only reminder that life still existed as it provided a graph that moved in a blip across the screen.

It was thirty-three minutes later that the graph changed to a flat green line. Billy was truly gone, now a part of eternity.

❧

As they stood in the hallway outside Billy's room, Dan said to the doctor, "We've been rethinking the possibility of Billy becoming a donor. What, specifically, must be done?"

"I'll get the necessary paperwork for you," he said. "I'll only be a minute or two."

When the doctor returned, the pair signed the forms and returned them to the doctor.

"What next?" Dan asked, while wondering when, if ever, this nightmare would finally end.

"The next thing for you to do is to make final preparations for burial or cremation," the doctor said. "Please tell the funeral director that Billy is going to be an organ donor. That will be taken into consideration when making burial or cremation plans."

CHAPTER 17

The End of an Era

A combined visitation and memorial service was scheduled for Billy. It was to take place on a sunny Friday afternoon from 2:00 to 4:00 p.m. at the funeral home. However, the turnout from Billy's classmates was so overwhelming that it was extended until 6:00 p.m. A simple, yet elegant urn stood on a long table at the end of the room. Next to it were dozens of framed pictures of Billy, from shortly after birth, celebrating birthdays, accepting diving and swimming trophies, pictures with Foxy Lady, pictures of all kinds.

Every seat was occupied in the funeral home and the line of visitors was more than a city block long for most of that time. Although an obituary that appeared in the daily newspaper suggested, "No flowers, please. Contributions may be made to your local ASPCA in the name of 'William Cooper,' if desired," the visitation room was filled with flowers of every type. They were sent by relatives, classmates, teachers, and neighbors. Billy was greatly loved and respected—that could not be denied. He was a good kid who was so easygoing that it would have been difficult to not like him.

The deep aroma of flowers wafted out of the visitation room, outside where incoming visitors were greeted by the fragrance long before they entered the funeral home.

Billy's grandparents had arrived late in the evening on the day the boy died, and it was evident that his death had taken its toll on both of them. "Dear, dear Danny and Cathy," Anne said, embracing the duo at the same time, "you know how very much Billy meant to us," as they sat next to the bereaved parents in the funeral home.

Cried out for the moment, Cathy could only nod in response. A red-eyed Dan replied simply, "We know, Mom, we know."

Cathy finally whispered to her parents, "I don't remember if we told you, but Billy's become an organ donor in death." That term, "in death," sounded so strange, so unnatural and cruel to Cathy.

"Yes, Dan told us," Anne replied for both. "Even in death he continues to make us proud."

By 6:30 p.m., the crowds had dispersed.

The small family remained to say a final goodbye to their son and grandson, whose cremains were then taken in a small solemn motorcade to local cemetery's memorial garden where they were placed in a niche. A small bronze plaque was placed on the stone that sealed the niche:

~~William Bertram Cooper~~
1967–1982
Beloved Son

It was done. Billy had assumed his rightful place in history.

CHAPTER 18

An Unaccepted Plan

Dan turned forty-five in 1985. Cathy would be turning forty-three soon. Everyday life had not gone easily since Billy's untimely death. Cathy withdrew and was living in a world of her own. She visited the cemetery almost every day to spend time with their son, sometimes remaining for hours at a time. In pleasant weather she'd sit on the ground next to his memorial. If it rained, she would sit in her car, staring at the site. She was clearly over-despondent and no amount of Dan's prodding that she should consider seeing a mental health specialist worked. She was adamant that she was "fine" and not some "mental case."

Dan attempted to add some "life" into the house by surprising Cathy with a puppy, a wire haired fox terrier in 1983. She went into a rage at the thought of a dog replacing her son. Dan returned the dog and vowed to himself not to attempt such a suggestion again.

Dan was promoted again. He was now in complete charge of the display advertising department of the newspaper. As he sat at his desk one afternoon, he realized that both of them could use a vacation. Remembering their plans to go on a delayed honeymoon for their twenty-fifth anniversary, he decided to take the initiative and plan on taking one this year, hopefully within a few months.

They needed to get away, and with his current position they could certainly afford it.

He called home to get Cathy's input on the idea. The phone went unanswered. *She's probably at the cemetery,* Dan thought, realizing that her preoccupation with Billy and her constant visits were becoming a greater issue to her mental well-being. An occasional visit on specific holidays would be fine, but she was obsessed with visiting Billy. Although she took care of herself, she had begun to look older than her years, haggard and worn out.

When Dan arrived home from work, he expected to find the aroma of food cooking in the kitchen. The house was empty, however. If she had been visiting Billy, Cathy still was not home. It was nearly six.

As Dan got back in his car to take the short ride to the cemetery, Cathy came driving up the driveway.

"I was worried about you, hon," Dan said, exiting his car and kissing her on the cheek.

"Worried? Why in the world would you worry? I'm a big girl now, Danny," she replied.

Dan sensed the caustic tone in her voice, but he didn't address it as he followed Cathy into the house.

"Hon, I was thinking at work today about taking an 'early' late honeymoon/vacation. We certainly can afford to do it now rather than put it on hold for another four years until our twenty-fifth anniversary." He added, "What do you think?"

"I'm in no hurry," Cathy replied. "I haven't even thought about that since Billy …" stopping abruptly, then continuing, "… for a long time."

"Cath, what you're doing by visiting Billy every day is taking its toll on you, you know. It's not normal, and it's not healthy for you."

"Dan, he was our son! How can you possibly think that I should abandon him or his memory?" demanded an infuriated Cathy.

"Cathy, I'm not saying that you should 'abandon' him. He was my son, too, and I loved him and miss him every bit as much as you do, but life must go on," a weary Dan replied. "I think about Billy constantly, but I do my best to occupy myself in ways that I don't dwell on him. It's simply not healthy. He's gone and nothing can … nothing will change that fact. Cathy, please, if you'll consider seeing a psychiatrist and pour out your heart and soul to him I'll be right there with you. I won't let you down."

Cathy bolted from the room and ran back out to the car.

Returning back to the house, she slapped a box containing a pizza down on the island countertop. "Supper," she said as she withdrew to the bedroom to change.

Shaking his head, partly in anger but mainly in disappointment, Dan sat down on a bar stool in front of the unopened pizza. Toying with the a flap on the box, his mind wandered back to another day, the day Billy suggested getting a "pizzeria pizza" in an effort to get an ailing Foxy Lady to eat. She ate part of a single slice that day. Dan wanted none today. His mind drifted further back in time, reliving portions of the past few years. Too many changes had taken place. Life was not easy. Would it ever be normal again? Was it a lack of faith? Was it that failure that he was being punished for neglecting? Dan questioned himself, but he could not come up with an answer.

∽✲∾

"I'm sorry," a repentant Cathy said as she meekly reentered the kitchen. "Danny, I'm simply so tired. I feel so … defeated … so useless."

"I know, Cath. I know." Dan replied. "But you must know that I'm experiencing the same pain as you. I fight it, Cath. I keep busy. Have you ever considered becoming a volunteer in the pediatrics area of the hospital, or with a Boys or Girls Club? Or a den mother for a Girl Scouts group? Activities like that could help keep you physically and mentally occupied. Think about it, you'd be doing something positive for children who might lack support from their own parents. It could give you a sense of wellbeing, give you a reason for living, and make you a role-model for children in need. The Cathy that I know and love would be a perfect role-model!" Dan added, "Or, you could even think of getting a part-time job where you'd be surrounded by other people. God knows we don't need the extra income, but if it would help you to be …"

"Normal?" Cathy replied sarcastically.

"To be kept busy, Cathy. Be reasonable. You know that isn't what I meant," Dan said. "I'm only trying to make things easier for you. Cathy, I love you more than you'll ever know, but your preoccupation with Billy is not doing any good for either of us."

"Have some pizza," she replied. "I'm fine."

"I'm not hungry," an equally upset Dan replied.

"Then toss it. I don't want any either," Cathy countered.

It was the only night in more than twenty-one years that the couple didn't kiss before going to sleep. It was the only night that they slept in different rooms. It was the only night that they went to bed angry.

CHAPTER 19

The '80s End

The remainder of the '80s had its ups and downs. Cathy's dad died in 1987 at the age of seventy-one. He died doing what he loved most—well, second-most. His first love was Anne. He suffered a massive stroke and died while golfing. His death took a major toll on Cathy.

At the funeral, Anne lovingly placed his putting iron by his side in the casket, at the ready in the event there were golf courses in heaven. To its side was a neatly folded loud, flowered Hawaiian shirt and his newest visor cap.

Anne followed her husband in 1989. She was seventy. She simply "fell asleep." There was no pain, no suffering. Except for Dan, Cathy, and a small circle of friends, there were few to mourn Bill and Anne's deaths. It was another blow for Cathy's mental well-being. She was becoming increasingly preoccupied with thoughts of her own death. It was almost as if she welcomed the idea.

Dan turned forty-nine; Cathy was forty-seven.

Over the years since Billy's death, Cathy's mental state suffered. She constantly punished herself with her near-daily visits to the cemetery. She became careless with her driving. Several times she was nearly broadsided as she made the left turn from the cemetery onto the main street on her way home, failing to pay attention to the oncoming traffic. Dan was surprised, in her depressed state, that she had even mentioned those incidents to him. He repeatedly suggested things that she could do to keep occupied. Each suggestion was met with a curt dismissal: "I'm fine, Dan."

The once stunningly beautiful Cathy had aged prematurely, looking more like a sixty-five-year-old retiree than the wife of the still handsome Dan, who, except for a few "age lines" and steely-gray temples looked years younger than forty-nine. Her hair had turned totally gray, and it had lost the sheen and body of youth. Her face and upper body however, were tan, a tan maintained by her near-daily visits to Bill sitting in the sun. Yet, she was fragile; she seldom wore a smile and rarely makeup. She went about her housework like a robot, often putting daily routines off until "next time." She had lost all interest in life except for her visits with Billy.

In a few weeks, the year and the decade would end. Dan decided that it was time for a change. He made plans to celebrate the new year/decade by having a late dinner in the clubhouse of one of the city's golf courses, followed by a New Year's Eve celebration in the same clubhouse. The year would change, the decade would change, and by damn, the remainder of their lives would change, too! It had to. The mourning had gone on far too long, and the pressure was becoming unbearable.

"Cathy," he announced as he entered the kitchen where she, surprisingly, was actually cooking. "I want you to get out shopping for a special New Year's Eve outfit. And make an appointment at the salon to have your hair colored and nails done. We're going out on New Year's Eve. That afternoon we're going to visit Billy together." Cautiously, he added, "And I'll be happy to help you pick out a special stand-out outfit."

Cathy responded "Fine, sure," without looking up from the salad she was preparing. She had a "Cathy special," lasagna, in the oven. The room was filled with the aroma of a freshly baked loaf of homemade garlic bread. It was a pleasant, warm aroma. "Where will we be going?"

"To the golf course clubhouse," Dan replied. "We'll have a late dinner there and stay for the midnight celebration," he added. "You and I both know it'll do us both good to get out among other people and we might actually enjoy it. It's been far too long, Cath."

"We might," Cathy said, "but for now, it's almost time to eat. Would you please get ready?"

Cathy's attitude both pleased and disturbed Dan at the same time. *That was too easy*, he thought, but his pleased side quickly dismissed the thought.

They both sat down to a pleasant meal. Cathy even ate more than usual.

CHAPTER 20

The Transformation

New Year's Eve and New Year's Day were holidays at the newspaper. The staff consisted of a skeleton crew; however, department heads were expected to be "on call" in the event of emergencies. Dan hoped there would be no emergencies for him on New Year's Eve.

Cathy had gone shopping for a new outfit earlier that week: gown, shoes, handbag, and some "baubles" as Dan called her jewelry. Dan joined her and highly approved of her choices. Her gown was pale yellow silky Grecian-styled, with a high waistline that high-lighted her breasts and its pale color emphasized her tan. It had a multitude of pleats and folds that fell dra-matically to the floor, forming a puddle at her feet. It was stunning; Cathy was stunning as she whirled, form-ing billows with the fabric, smiling ever so slightly and almost feeling guilty all the while.

She chose a simple see-through shawl in a lighter shade of pale yellow to carry over her arm: insurance against the possibility of a cool evening. A choke neck-lace and earrings of black imitation pearls, a tiny black sequined clutch purse and black sequined toeless heels completed the outfit.

That morning, December 31, 1989, Cathy went to the beauty parlor. It had been years since she had indulged herself, although cost had not been an issue.

Her hair was shampooed, and then colored with her natural shade of ash blonde. Then it was trimmed and shampooed a second time. At the same time her hair was being attended to, a manicurist provided a manicure and pedicure. A pearl-colored nail polish provided the finishing touch. Finally, her eyebrows were plucked, formed into a high arch. A slight application of mascara accentuated her blue eyes even further, if that were possible.

As she left the salon, passersby turned to take a second look at Cathy. She could have passed for an older, blonde Audrey Hepburn, her hair tightly pulled back in a chignon with wispy, soft curling ringlets framing her glowing face at the sides. She looked good; she actually felt good. She was pleased. Dan would be pleased, but more importantly, soon she and Dan would be going to visit Billy.

❧

Dan was busy working in the front lawn when Cathy turned into the driveway. He glanced up and did a double-take as she got out of the car.

She was positively stunning!

"Wow!" he exclaimed, getting up and walking toward her. He was about to hug her when he realized that his hands were gritty with sandy soil. Instead, he leaned over and gently kissed her cheek first, then lips. "You look amazing, honey!"

Cathy simply smiled a broad smile, tweaked him under the chin and continued toward the door. Dan followed.

Cathy busied herself by preparing a small picnic lunch to take to the cemetery. There was a small gazebo close to the spot where Billy's ashes had been placed. They could have a late lunch near their son. She made two sandwiches and carefully wrapped them. Then she placed some ice cubes into a plastic bag, added small containers of olives, pickles, and an assortment of diced fresh fruits: grapes, watermelon, and cantaloupe, and a small bag of potato chips, humming softly as she moved along, placing several soft drinks into a cooler half filled with ice. As an afterthought, she took a plastic tablecloth, folded it, and took a few paper napkins and placed them on top of the basket along with two small paper bowls, two plastic spoons and two paper dinner plates.

CHAPTER 21

A Visit with Billy

Dan and Cathy arrived at the memorial garden shortly after 2:00 p.m., parked the car, and walked the short distance to Billy's final resting place. Dan placed the picnic basket on the table under the gazebo, and they walked a few feet further to visit with Billy. It was a sunny day, but very pleasant with a gentle breeze blowing inland from the Gulf of Mexico.

Both stood for a few minutes not saying a word. Then they moved to a small concrete bench and Dan broke the silence. "Cathy, I know how much you miss Billy. I do, too. But honestly, we need to get on with our lives. I'll never stop loving Billy, and I know you won't either. It's time to 'let go,' now. That doesn't mean that Billy will be forgotten. You're a woman of deep faith, and in your heart you know that someday we'll all meet again, and we will never be separated."

Cathy didn't reply, but she nodded in agreement. Her hands folded gently on her lap, she felt a tear fall from her eye. She didn't bother to wipe it away. It deserved to be there. It was expressing her feelings at the moment. It was a tear formed especially for Billy.

They got up from the bench and walked to the gazebo. Billy's resting place was still in their view as Dan unpacked the basket. He spread the tablecloth on the table, along with the napkins and spoons. Finally he took the wrapped sandwiches, placing one atop a paper plate on Cathy's side of the table and one on his, adding one of the small bowls to hold the fresh fruits. He placed a small handful of chips on each plate and added a pickle and a few olives to each. They ate mostly in silence. The cool ham and Swiss was perfect for a warm day; the entire meal was refreshing.

At about 3:30 p.m., Dan suggested that they return home. Cathy began to object, but she relented and they cleared the table and drove off.

After leaving the cemetery, the couple returned home. Dan put the picnic gear in its place and both went to the lanai to unwind before getting ready for the New Year's Eve celebration. The skimmer of the swimming pool provided just enough background sound as the water gently splashed against the sides of the pool. Dan finished the morning paper as Cathy simply relaxed on a chaise lounge. Both were dozing in less than a half hour.

At around 5:00 p.m., Dan was awakened by the buzz of an insect that was hovering near his ear. He looked at his watch. Scooping up the newspaper he walked over to Cathy's chaise and kissed her on her forehead saying, "Time to start getting ready, Cathy."

She stirred, trying to avoid moving. It was so relaxing lying there, but soon it would turn cool as the sun set. Reluctantly she rose, took her towel and went into the house, closely followed by Dan, who closed and locked the triple sliders that separated the house from the lanai.

They nibbled on a small snack since they would be having a late dinner at the golf course.

CHAPTER 22

New Year's Eve

Dan and Cathy arrived at the clubhouse shortly after 8:00 p.m., a "fashionable" time for a New Year's Eve dinner and celebration. They were greeted by numerous mutual friends, all of whom stared in amazement at a beautifully transformed Cathy, who looked radiant with her hairdo and new outfit. She positively glowed. Inwardly, Dan also glowed … with pride.

They were seated at a table for eight with three other couples whom Cathy hadn't seen in several years. The clubhouse was filled to its legal capacity, and its holiday centerpieces and decorations were outstanding. It was a perfect setting for a perfect celebration; a perfect new outlook on life.

Their small talk added to the strains of soft holiday music streaming from speakers that surrounded the room. The live band was scheduled to begin performing for three hours starting at 10:00 p.m.

The couples ordered cocktails from the waitress whose station included their table along with several others. Dan had a gin and tonic with lime, while Cathy opted for straight tonic water with a slice of lime and ice cubes. She, like Dan's stepmother/mother, was not especially fond of alcohol, although she took a drink from time to time.

Small talk continued as the partygoers awaited the start of the live band and dancing. Surprisingly Cathy was somewhat animated as she joined in the conversation, mostly "girl talk" with the other women at the table, although from time to time she placed her hand on Dan's and smiled sweetly at him. He was still the most important person in her life. That would never change—never. For a brief moment Cathy regretted that she disappointed him with her ongoing visits with Billy, but that brief moment passed as she mentally planned her next visit with their son.

She pleased Dan, not once referring to Billy. That was a good sign. She appeared to be honestly enjoying herself: another good sign. It was good for her to be spending time with the girls. *She might even start to be more outgoing after tonight,* Dan thought.

As the band started to play, all over the room couples rose to go to the dance floor, Dan and Cathy among them. "This feels so good, you in my arms again," Dan said as he kissed her lightly on the neck.

"It does," Cathy replied, looking up into his brilliant green eyes.

They danced to several slow songs, withdrawing to their table as the band began playing a tango. They were a bit too rusty to attempt it; however, they enjoyed watching some of the more proficient dancers as they circled the floor with dramatic moves and footwork. Several were really good.

Dan carefully placed the see-through pale yellow shawl over Cathy's shoulders when they decided to walk outside to say "goodbye" to December 1989. A new decade would begin shortly; a decade that he

CROSSING THE RAINBOW BRIDGE

hoped would return some 'normalcy' to their lives. He craved that so badly.

Dan handed Cathy a fresh glass of iced tonic water with a slice of lime as he raised his third gin and tonic of the evening, "To the '90s—a new year and a new decade," he said as their glasses touched.

"To the '90s," Cathy replied, looking more beautiful than ever in the light of a waning moon. "To better days and a better decade," she added, as their glasses touched a second time.

They kissed and moments later they walked back inside.

"Ten, nine, eight, seven, six, five, four, three, two, one: HAPPY NEW YEAR!" the crowd shouted in a countdown to 1990.

Dan and Cathy were seated at their table while the other couples mingled on the dance floor or at the bar, and table-hopped while extending "Happy New Year" wishes to both friends and strangers alike.

A stranger who had a few too many drinks stumbled up to the table and loudly blew a tinny-sounding horn behind Cathy's ear in an attempt to add to the general merriment as he yelled, "Happy New Year!"

A startled Cathy jumped up from her seat by reflex rather than intent, turning to the man as she pushed the horn from his mouth, knocking it out of his hand at the same time shouting, "No! No, no, NO! This isn't real! It's all a lie! I'm just imagining this!"

She turned and ran toward the exit door as she slipped and fell on the dance floor, screaming all the time, "No! No! No!" Rising off the floor she slipped again. She removed her heels and tossed them to the side and ran outside barefooted as the other partygoers looked at her in shock. They began whispering among themselves.

Racing after her, a shocked Dan finally caught up with her and held her tightly in his arms. "Hon, what is it? What's wrong?" he asked.

She didn't reply. She didn't say a word, but instinctively Dan knew that something horrible was happening. He was holding her, but her arms hung limply at her side. She was like a puppet without strings.

After several minutes without response, he looked into her lifeless blue eyes. He carried her to the car and drove to the hospital emergency room.

CHAPTER 23

A Disturbing Turn

Fortunately for them, most people were still out party-ing or celebrating at home. The new year was less than an hour old, and in another hour there would prob-ably be dozens of people waiting for treatment from minor accidents, injuries from errant fireworks that prematurely exploded, fender-benders and the like. It happened every New Year's Eve and New Year's Day. But for now, the waiting room was empty except for hospital employees.

After a lengthy physical exam, the ER doctor in charge called a staff psychiatrist who was on call, ask-ing him to report to the hospital as soon as possible.

"She appears to be catatonic," the ER doctor said to Dan. "Has anything unusual happened recently?"

Dan related what had taken place at the party, add-ing his perception of Cathy's preoccupation with Billy's death nearly eight years earlier as well as her constant, almost daily visits to his final resting place. "Regardless of the weather, she'll spend hours some days 'visiting' with him," Dan said. "Yet, yesterday I went with her and everything appeared to be perfectly normal. As a matter of fact, everything appeared normal until that guy blew the horn into her ear. That seems to have set her off. She hasn't uttered a word since we left the clubhouse."

The staff psychiatrist arrived moments later dressed in a tuxedo. It was clear that his partying had been interrupted. Along with the ER staff, he began a series of intensive tests on Cathy, among them a brain scan, pain reflex tests and more.

Cathy was admitted to the hospital on the first day of January, 1990.

In the days that followed, more and more tests were taken and more specialists were called in. All of the doctors involved came up with one conclusion: Cathy had given up; she had no desire to live. She appeared to be welcoming the very thing she feared: an early death.

When presented with the facts, it was suggested to Dan that she be placed in a private medical facility where she could be cared for and continue to be treated, if possible. It was a heart-wrenching decision to make; however, Dan had no choice. He could not quit his job and neither he nor Cathy had any family that could help if she were to remain at home. Successful as he was, it would not be possible to hire private-duty nurses for in-home care.

A week later, Cathy was transported to a private rehabilitation facility that would, at least for now, become her new home. She showed no signs of concern or upset when she was taken to the small but bright room. There was no response when she was introduced to the nurse that was on duty. Likewise, there was no response when Dan kissed her and left to return home. Cathy had failed to respond to anything at all since that fateful January 1. It appeared that her premonitions, her thoughts and preoccupation with an early death might indeed become fact.

CHAPTER 24

Necessary Measures

It was more than a month since Cathy entered the rehabilitation facility, and there was no change in her condition. She could not eat by herself. She had to be fed by staff. Most of the time she would turn her face away from the food that was offered to her. She lost weight, and her features were startling. Her hair, which had been colored barely a month ago, was lifeless, perhaps the result of medications. The color was now growing out.

Dan visited her every day after work and spent most of his Saturdays and Sundays with her, taking time off only to do the necessary tasks at home: mowing the lawn, laundry, and the like.

He resolved himself to the fact that most likely Cathy would never be returning home, and if by some miracle she would be able to do so, she would never be able to manage so large a home. He was becoming run-down in his efforts to be the loving husband, yet he persisted.

He decided to put the house up for sale. He contracted with a real estate agent to look for a first floor condo with two bedrooms and two baths (in the event

Cathy would ever return home). He wanted to be sure that she would not have to contend with stairs to a second- or third-floor condo. He spent a good deal of his spare time looking at properties the agent referred to him.

Early in March, Dan found a condo that he felt would be suitable for him as well as Cathy. Their home had not yet sold, but several open houses looked promising. He was able to pay the mortgage off early so there would be no hardship in owning two homes until it sold. He was free to move into the condo immediately, so he advertised items for sale that he would not be taking to the condo: furniture from the third and fourth bedrooms, the lawn mower, and more.

Dan moved out of their home in mid-March, settling into the condo. It seemed strange, after having a home of his (their) own for nearly thirty years, to be confined to the relative smallness of a condo, yet the fact that there was less to do there and no outdoor maintenance freed him to spend more time with Cathy.

Months passed, then years, and Cathy did not improve. It truly appeared that she was trying to embrace death—and she achieved her goal.

In May 1995, shortly before Mother's Day, Dan got a call from the rehabilitation home. Cathy had passed on early that morning. The night-shift nurse was just going off duty, and the nurse for the seven to three shift entered the room preparing for a new day. As she opened the blinds, she glanced toward Cathy's bed. There was no need to rush, no need to call for help. She could see from Cathy's open, sightless eyes that the woman was dead. She buzzed the staff doctor who entered the room, checked for vital signs, and pronounced her dead at 7:05 a.m. Cathy was only fifty-three.

CHAPTER 25

Retirement and Plans for a New Friend

The years passed slowly. It was 2002, and Dan, at age sixty-two, decided to take an early retirement. With his savings, a company pension, and an IRA to draw from, he determined that he would have no financial hardship by not applying for Social Security until he reached age sixty-six. The laws had changed, and he would have to wait an added year in order to qualify for full retirement benefits. He wasn't concerned.

But he was lonely. After Cathy died, he found himself visiting her and Billy most weekends. When he returned home, he realized that it appeared quieter in the condo than it was at the cemetery. He genuinely missed signs of life. The radio or TV did little to add to the life that he needed to surround him. Dan decided to get a puppy. Small dogs were permitted by the condo association. Living on the first floor, there would be no difficulty taking a dog outside to do its duty. He would not disturb other residents in doing so.

There was also a beach in Venice that permitted dogs. *Yes*, Dan thought to himself, smiling, *I'll get a roommate.*

A few days later Dan stopped by the Sunnyside Animal Hospital. He realized that at age sixty-two, there was a very good chance that a new puppy could easily outlive him. The last thing he would want is for an orphaned dog to be euthanized because its owner had died and nobody else would want it. He explained his predicament to the manager of the facility, who listened intently.

"You know, Mr. Cooper, you could always make provisions in your will, providing for the care of your pet. It could be entrusted to the ASPCA to provide financial assistance for its care. Or, you could sign a legal agreement with an individual whom you feel you could trust to provide the care that you would want for your pet," she said. "A specific bank account could be set up for that purpose."

"That's a wonderful idea!" Dan said, smiling from ear to ear. "I know that your co-worker Kaitlin is a great animal lover. She once told my wife about her menagerie. Is she still with Sunnyside?"

"Oh, I'm afraid she's not, Mr. Cooper. She hasn't been with us for many years. She continued with her education and has since become a veterinarian. She probably left here about fifteen years ago. She married and has her own business about twelve miles from here. I'm told that she still has a 'menagerie.'"

"May I have the address of her business?" Dan asked. "She could well be the person to consider!"

"Of course," the receptionist replied. She handed him one of Kaitlin's cards. "Here it is."

"Thanks very much," Dan said, as he prepared to leave.

"You're welcome, Mr. Cooper," she replied, adding, "Have you decided on a specific breed?"

"Yes, as a matter of fact, I have. I'm planning to get a wire-haired fox terrier—just like one that my son once saw on TV; just like Foxy Lady."

"That's great," she replied. "They are a wonderful breed!"

Dan thanked her again and returned home to make plans for welcoming his new roommate.

❦

From the comfort of his living room, he dialed Kaitlin's number and identified himself. He assumed that she'd be busy, so he asked the receptionist to have her call him at her convenience. "Please tell her that the reason for my call is a possible business venture," he added cryptically as he thought, *I hope she doesn't think that I'm some kind of nut.*

Thanking the receptionist, he hung up the phone. He picked up the local paper and opened it to the pet section. There were no fox terriers for sale or adoption. He might have to advertise as he did for Billy's Foxy Lady, but first he decided to surf the Internet for "female wire haired fox terriers in Southwest Florida."

Bingo! Dan said to himself as the Web search produced a page advertising wire haired fox terriers in Naples, Florida, which was only about sixty miles to the south. He printed all pages that advertised a female. It was a start!

Dan sat back on his computer chair looking at the printouts. Some of them were rescue dogs awaiting adoption at their local animal shelter, some were being offered, he was certain, by puppy mill breeders. They were all so cute!

His reverie was broken by the sound of the ringing of the phone, which seldom rang anymore.

"Hello," he said, picking up the phone.

"Mr. Cooper," the voice on the other end said, "This is Dr.—"

"Ah, Kaitlin," he said, thoughtlessly interrupting, it occurred to him.

"Yes. How are you Mr. Cooper?" she asked. "I've thought about you folks many times over the years and the great love you all had for Foxy Lady."

"You remember her?" Dan asked. *How strange, after all the years that had passed that Kaitlin still remembered them,* he thought.

"Of course I do. I was so sorry to hear of Billy and your wife's deaths," she replied. "Foxy Lady was one of my favorite clients. I don't think that I could ever forget her."

She's the one, Dan thought excitedly. *If my new fox terrier has to leave me, she certainly is the one to care for her.* "Kaitlin, I have a proposition to make to you. Don't be alarmed. It's strictly a business proposition."

Kaitlin chuckled on the other end of the line. "Of course," she said, "Propose on!"

Dan revealed his plan to her, and he was thrilled that she thought it was an idea with merit.

"And I'd provide sufficient funds to care for her needs for the rest of her life," he explained further after outlining his plan, "as well as a stipend for you for being the caretaker, or, I should say, for taking on the responsibility for her care."

"Mr. Cooper, I'm truly honored that you would entrust me with so great a responsibility. I'd be more than happy to accept," Kaitlin said.

"Thank you so much, Kaitlin. You have no idea how much this means to me. I'll feel so much better knowing that if I were to die, my new roommate will be cared for. You've taken a great weight off my mind. I'll speak with my attorney first thing in the morning and have him get back to you with the details." Dan was almost in tears with gratitude.

"Fine, Mr. Cooper. I'll look forward to discussing this 'venture' with him," she replied. "You have a good night now, hear?"

"Please call me 'Dan,'" he said. "After all, we're almost family now, aren't we?"

"Sure thing, Dan," Kaitlin replied.

Both chuckled as they hung up their phones.

Dan made a mental note to change veterinarians as he lay in bed. He was happy as sleep began to close in on him, making a second mental note to make Kaitlin his sole heir since he had no other survivors. His attorney would take care of everything. That was his job. He slept well that night—better than he had in a long, long time. Dan had something to look forward to—a new roommate!

CHAPTER 26

Lady II: A Grand Entrance

After several weeks of searching, Dan finally located a female wire haired fox terrier, a pup only six weeks old. She was a beauty, and he accepted her on the spot. As he picked her up for the first time and held her to his chest, she licked his face and peed down his shirt. It was an instant bonding! He was required to wait an additional two weeks before he could claim her and take her home. Those two weeks passed ever so slowly.

He spent much of that time accumulating the things every puppy needs: shiny new bowls for food and water, a leash, a tiny choke collar, food, toys, toys and more toys, and of course, a doggie bed that she'd possibly never use, as well as a crate. His joy in anticipation of a new friend, a roommate, had him smiling constantly.

The day finally arrived. He drove to Naples to claim his new friend. On the ride back, "Lady II" claimed the console for her front feet with the back seat of the car supporting her rear. But she was too small to remain there, so she curled up on the passenger seat and went to sleep after first investigating every square inch of the seat.

They arrived home in a bit more than an hour. As they entered the condo, Lady found it difficult to scamper around on the tiled portions of the floor, instead finding herself sliding from here to there on her butt. She investigated every room carefully before discovering the water dish in the kitchen along with the food that Dan prepared for her. She ate every bit of it and though she looked for more, Dan didn't accommodate her. He would stick by the rules that Kaitlin established, and there would be no table scraps. Her treats would consist of fresh carrot sticks, celery and fresh fruit: nothing commercially prepared. He vowed to do everything in his power to prevent another disastrous kidney failure by feeding her improperly. At bedtime, it was as Dan had anticipated. With Lady's bed at the side of his bed, a ticking clock, and one of Dan's socks inside it, Lady began to whimper. She didn't want to be alone. Dan reached down, picked up the little bundle of fur, and placed her atop the spare pillow. She was not satisfied, however, until she dug and scratched, forming her own little niche in the pillow. Then she curled up and fell asleep facing Dan. It turned out to be a good day—a very good day indeed. Dan felt pleased as he drifted into the most comfortable slumber he'd had in years.

Each day brought new and exciting adventures for the duo: a stroll downtown; a romp in the Gulf at the puppy beach; a walk along the Intracoastal Waterway separating Venice from Venice Island (where Lady first learned to bark at the boats that went up and down the waterway); playing catch with the ball and an assortment of other toys in the small but ample backyard of the condo.

Dan began to feel alive again. It had been a long time since he looked forward to getting out of bed each morning, and by nighttime he was sufficiently played out to be able to fall asleep quickly without reliving the nightmares of years gone by. In the months that passed since Lady came into his life, she graduated from sleeping atop the pillow to a nightly ritual of digging and scratching a niche in the linens so that she could sleep in a spoon position next to Dan. Not a night went by that she failed to initiate a kissing session, kissing Dan's face so fiercely that he feared that he'd lose his breath. He would pat her gently on the head and simply say, "Okay, Lady, that's enough kissing. It's time to go to sleep now." As if she understood him, she'd curl up in her niche and go to sleep, not moving from that position until morning.

Dan and Lady's relationship continued to grow day by day. She matured into a beautiful dog, lean and strong. Their daily exercise regimens kept her trim while trimming some of the excess weight from Dan. They both looked great. However, Dan suffered a stroke in 2005, three years after he and Lady first met. He was only sixty-five.

CHAPTER 27

Kaitlin Enters the Picture

Dan was discovered when his next door neighbor and the neighbor above him heard Lady whining. The neighbors hadn't seen either Dan or Lady that day. That in itself was unusual. They were in the habit of getting up early to go for their morning walk before the sun became too hot to enjoy even the shortest walk.

After ringing the doorbell and calling his number without a response other than Lady's cries, the neighbors contacted the manager of the condo, who used a master key to enter the home. Dan was lying in bed, sweating profusely, unable to rise.

One of the neighbors quickly dialed 911, and an ambulance came to take Dan to the hospital. As the EMTs placed him on the stretcher, Dan pointed to a card on the nightstand. One of the EMTs picked up and read it asking, "Kaitlin? Do you want me to call this Kaitlin and tell her what happened?"

Dan nodded yes, got his breath back sufficiently to be able to say, "She'll know what must be done," in a slurred voice.

The EMT gave the card to one of the neighbors, asking her to place the call. "We need to get this man to the hospital," he explained.

"I understand," the neighbor replied. "I'll take care of it."

Arriving about forty minutes later, Kaitlin unlocked the door with the spare key Dan had provided for her. After feeding Lady and cleaning her dishes, she picked them up along with Lady's supply of food and took them to her car. She returned to claim a half-dozen of Lady's toys and placed them in the back seat. Then she put Lady's leash on and led her to the car. They went to Kaitlin's home.

Lady appeared to be lost in her strange surroundings. However, after a short time she began playing with some of the "menagerie," which consisted of several dogs, cats, birds (in cages, of course) and even some harmless snakes (in aquariums).

Kaitlin went to the hospital to visit Dan after work. He was stable, but very weak. The stroke had affected his left side as well as the left side of his face, making speaking clearly difficult. Smiling as much as he was able to he asked, "How's Lady?" with a slur to the "s." A series of wires were attached to him.

"She's just fine Dan. It will take some time for her to adjust to her surroundings, but she'll be fine, I'm sure, until you come home," the vet replied, adding, "I know that you miss her already."

"If I come home," Dan said.

"Now Dan, stop talking like that. You'll go through a period of rehab and you'll be just fine. Better than ever, probably," Kaitlin continued. "In the meantime, you can rest assured that Lady will be given loads of love and affection and she'll be kept occupied."

Dan nodded, smiled as well as he was able to, and with the aid of medications, he drifted off to a troubled sleep.

It was nearing dawn when Dan opened his eyes. Without moving his head, his eyes surveyed the dimly lit room. With a jolt, his body stiffened as he suffered another stroke—a fatal stroke. It lasted a brief moment. His earthly eyes closed one last time, in eternal sleep.

CHAPTER 28

Crossing the Rainbow Bridge

As Dan's eyes opened, he heard the sound of a babbling brook. He appeared to be in the midst of a green meadow filled with a fresh, clean morning mist, flowers in every direction, and birds singing softly as they darted from here to there. As he turned to look from left to right and back again, a dog came running his way. As the dog approached more closely, he realized that it was Sadie! Mere moments later another dog approached. Wagging his tail was his beloved Cosmo! Both dogs came directly to him and proceeded to kiss him incessantly. Suddenly a third dog joined them. It was Foxy Lady! Then he heard a voice.

"Dad? Dad? It's really you! I've been waiting for you for so long!"

It was Billy! As Dan extended his arms to embrace his son, he saw that the wrinkled hands of the old Dan were no longer wrinkled. They were the hands of a young man. The young arms embraced the boy and an overwhelming sense of love took over every fiber of Dan's being.

"Billy, oh Billy, how I've missed you, son!" Dan said. As he stood there staring at Billy another voice emerged from the dissipating morning mist.

"Dan, oh my dear Dan!" It was Cathy! As she appeared through the mist, he could see that the woman who had left her earthly bounds at age fifty-three appeared to be as young as the day they'd wed. They kissed and held each other in a long embrace.

"I never believed," said Dan, with a smile on his face and not a tear in his eyes. There would never be a need for tears again. "I never believed in the 'Rainbow Bridge,' but I truly never gave up hoping."

It was not possible, yet there he was with the most important people in his earthly life, together with his beloved canine friends.

Anxious to move along, Sadie led the way, followed closely by Cosmo and Foxy Lady all romping excitedly, barking, and turning around from time to time, making certain that their humans would never leave them again.

Taking the dogs' lead, Dan took Cathy's hand into his as he placed an arm across Billy's shoulder. Together, they crossed over the Rainbow Bridge—into Paradise.

EPILOGUE

Dan had no memory of Foxy Lady II. He would not. When her time came to leave the Earth she would not remember him. She would be anxiously awaiting her caretaker, Kaitlin, on this side of the Rainbow Bridge.

Believe …

CPSIA information can be obtained at www.ICGtesting.com
Printed in the USA
LVOW130249180313

324704LV00001B/17/P